She's not your type, Linc told himself.

But he recognized this feeling he had deep down inside: he was starting up with Kansas Daye whether she was his type or not.

What he didn't understand was why. Kansas was fresh-faced and bright as a spring day.

She was also his late wife's kid sister.

And the kind of woman a man didn't mess with unless he was looking for a *relationship*. And Linc wasn't, damn those big green eyes of hers.

A challenge—maybe that's what Kansas was. A challenge to get past that controlled surface and find out if there was a hot spring beneath it. Because Linc was betting there was. He was betting that if he kissed her full on the mouth, he'd taste a little of it.

And damn it to hell, he wanted to. B̶a̶d̶l̶y̶.

Dear Reader,

Welcome to Silhouette **Special Edition**...welcome to romance.

Some of your favorite authors are prepared to create a veritable feast of romance for you as we enter the sometimes-hectic holiday season.

Our THAT SPECIAL WOMAN! title for November is *Mail Order Cowboy* by Patricia Coughlin. Feisty and determined Allie Halston finds she has a weakness for a certain cowboy as she strives to tame her own parcel of the open West.

We stay in the West for A RANCHING FAMILY, a new series from Victoria Pade. The Heller siblings—Linc, Beth and Jackson—have a reputation for lassoing the unlikeliest of hearts. This month, meet Linc Heller in *Cowboy's Kin*. Continuing in November is Lisa Jackson's LOVE LETTERS. In *B Is For Baby*, we discover sometimes all it takes is a letter of love to rebuild the past.

Also in store this month are *When Morning Comes* by Christine Flynn, *Let's Make It Legal* by Trisha Alexander, and *The Greatest Gift of All* by Penny Richards. Penny has long been part of the Silhouette family as Bay Matthews, and now writes under her own name.

I hope you enjoy this book, and all of the stories to come. Happy Thanksgiving Day—all of us at Silhouette would like to wish you a happy holiday season!

Sincerely,

Tara Gavin
Senior Editor

Please address questions and book requests to:
Silhouette Reader Service
U.S.: 3010 Walden Ave., P.O. Box 1325, Buffalo, NY 14269
Canadian: P.O. Box 609, Fort Erie, Ont. L2A 5X3

VICTORIA PADE

COWBOY'S KIN

SPECIAL EDITION®

Published by Silhouette Books
America's Publisher of Contemporary Romance

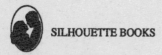

SILHOUETTE BOOKS

ISBN 0-373-09923-1

COWBOY'S KIN

Printed in U.S.A.

Books by Victoria Pade

Silhouette Special Edition

Breaking Every Rule #402
Divine Decadence #473
Shades and Shadows #502
Shelter from the Storm #527
Twice Shy #558
Something Special #600
Out on a Limb #629
The Right Time #689
Over Easy #710
Amazing Gracie #752
Hello Again #778
Unmarried with Children #852
*Cowboy's Kin #923

*A Ranching Family

VICTORIA PADE

is a bestselling author of both historical and contemporary romance fiction, and the mother of two energetic daughters, Cori and Erin. Although she enjoys her chosen career as a novelist, she occasionally laments that she has never traveled farther from her Colorado home than Disneyland, instead spending all her spare time plugging away at her computer. She takes breaks from writing by indulging in her favorite hobby—eating chocolate.

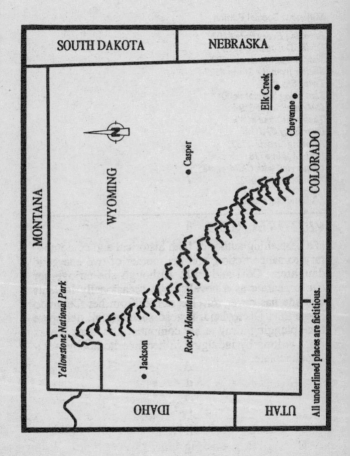

All underlined places are fictitious.

Chapter One

"This is WECW, ninety-five on your radio dial and servin' all of Elk Creek, Wyoming. To close out this end of May beauty of a day, I think we'll—"

The radio seemed to go dead, and though Kansas Daye had been talking to her sister Della and not really listening to it, that lack of sound made them both stop and stare at the small black portable that sat at the end of the counter in the old-fashioned country store Kansas owned.

"Well, I'll be damned," the disc jockey muttered then, sounding as if he'd seen a ghost.

"Bucky Dennehy," Della chastised as if her husband could hear her. "You know you're not supposed to swear on the air."

"If it isn't the missing Linc," he continued, really drawing their attention with that. "Old Hell-raiser Heller, stopped at the light right outside this station.

Didn't know you were back. How ya doin', boy? He's wavin' to me, folks, so I know he's listenin'. Must have just come in from the ranch—that where you been? Thought so. Well, welcome back," Bucky went on. "We're all sorry 'bout your daddy's passin', but it's good to see you. Think about stickin' around, would you? Ol' Elk Creek'd be glad to have you."

Della smacked the radio the way she might have hit her husband's arm were he within reach.

"Lincoln Heller is here?" Kansas said in disbelief, more to herself than to her older sister.

"Damn him, anyway," Della rumbled.

Kansas moved from behind the counter and headed for the big display window up front.

"Where are you going?" Della demanded.

"He could be coming down Center Street and might have Virgie's boy with him," she said, knowing she was wearing her heart on her sleeve and not caring.

"Don't go getting your hopes up," Della warned like a worried mother hen. "That baby must be nearly three years old by now. He doesn't know us and I doubt if Linc Heller will stay in town long enough for us to even be introduced, nephew or not. He'll hear what he's inherited from his cantankerous father and be off again looking for the next rodeo ride and the next roadhouse to kick up his heels in."

Kansas went to the window anyway.

At first her focus was on her own reflection in the glass. That was when she realized she was still wearing the round glasses she'd needed to see the small print on the order form she'd been checking against that morning's shipment of boxes.

She snatched them off and rubbed the bridge of her thin nose to remove the marks they'd left between her green eyes. Carefully she folded the temples and slipped them into the breast pocket of the crisp white shirt she wore buttoned to her throat, with the sleeves rolled meticulously up above her elbows and the tails tucked into her slightly baggy but freshly pressed jeans.

Then she smoothed the few strands of dark auburn hair straying from the braid that fell long past her shoulder blades, and she craned over the display of home-canned peaches, looking up Center Street toward the north of town, where the radio station was.

"Lord, he couldn't have come back at a worse time," she heard her sister mutter as Della came out from behind the counter, too. When she was nearer to Kansas, she said, "You better keep this in perspective. You're vulnerable right now where babies are concerned and—"

"You can't tell me you don't care about seeing Virgie's only child—the only nephew you'll ever have—"

"Don't talk like that. You could still have kids in your life. You could adopt. And they'd be as much my nieces and nephews as that boy Virginia didn't even have the decency to tell us about. Why, we might never have even known he existed if she were still alive and gallivanting around the country with Lincoln Heller."

"But we do know he exists and he's our own flesh and blood. Danny. She named him after old Granddad. It shows she was thinking about the family even if she didn't keep any contact with us," Kansas said, straightening up for a moment to face her sister with her conviction.

"Maybe Linc wouldn't let Virgie get in touch with us all those years or even tell us about the baby when she had him," Della postulated suspiciously.

"Or maybe Linc Heller didn't have anything to do with it. Maybe Virgie's leaving was so ugly and she said such awful things to Mama and Daddy that she was too ashamed to call or visit or even write. How else do you explain why she wouldn't come back even when Linc did for those six months to help when Jackson was gored by that bull? Six months, Della—she chose to be separated from her own husband for all that time rather than come here."

"That was eight years ago," Della answered as if it were too much before Danny's birth to matter.

"The point is, he certainly wasn't keeping her away then, and she still didn't come. I know how it hurt you that she didn't, but that's the truth of it and I don't think it's right to blame someone else for what our sister did."

"It didn't hurt me that she didn't come," Della denied too softly.

But Kansas knew better. Della and Virgie had been only a year apart in age and they'd been as close as twins. Kansas, who was seven years younger, had had a different relationship with Virgie, one that had left her with fewer illusions.

Kansas replaced her hands on the rod that held red-and-white-checked curtains as a half backdrop to her display and once again leaned as far over it as her short height allowed. "All I know is this is the first chance we've had to meet Danny and I'll do about anything to get to."

"Well, I just don't want you to forget the boy is half Lincoln Heller's," Della went on, "and he'll probably take him away again before you can blink twice. So don't go getting your hopes up over having anything much to do with that child."

"Danny. His name is Danny," Kansas said. "And quit your grumbling, because I know you want to see him as much as I do."

"Not if it means I have to set eyes on Linc Heller to do it. If it wasn't for him, Virgie might still be alive."

"We don't know that. We don't know anything except that Virgie was killed nearly three years ago in a bad car accident that Linc was hurt in, too. And that, thank God, the baby wasn't with them at the time," Kansas reminded as she watched for signs of her nephew.

"Why are you defending Linc Heller of all people?"

"Was I defending him?"

"It sure sounded like it. You wouldn't still be harboring that old crush on him, would you?"

Kansas glanced over her shoulder. "Do you really think I've been secretly pining for Linc Heller since I was a twelve-year-old kid, for crying out loud?"

"Stranger things have been known to happen."

"Including that you never took your eyes off him whenever he was around the house back then," she reminded. Then she shook her head. "No, Della, I have not been carrying a torch for Linc Heller for the past eighteen years, so you can relax. It's just Danny I want to see." Kansas went back to looking out the window.

For a moment neither of them said anything. Then, as if she were thinking aloud, Della said, "I wonder if he got married again."

That thought deflated some of Kansas's spirits. Somehow the idea of another woman taking over as her nephew's mother made the boy seem even further removed from their side of the family. "I don't know," she answered quietly. But it seemed like a strong possibility. After all, Virgie had died a long time ago and, unless he'd changed an awful lot, Linc Heller was not a man with a shortage of admiring females who could fill her place.

"I see a bright red pickup truck coming," Kansas announced then, spotting it far off in the distance. "Nobody around here drives one—it must be Linc's."

She could feel her sister's begrudging curiosity as the taller Della stepped up close behind her to see over her shoulder.

"A fire-engine-red truck. Leave it to him to drive a thing like that," Della said under her breath.

Just then the mayor's wife came through the store's front door, setting off the bell that hung over it and making both Kansas and Della jump.

"What are you girls doing?" Bernice Watson asked bluntly.

"Oh, nothing really," Della answered.

"We just heard Linc Heller is back in town and thought we might catch sight of our nephew," Kansas put in hopefully, still looking out the window.

"Oh, that's right. I heard Virginia left a little boy." The elderly, portly woman took up a spot next to Kansas and Della, peering around Kansas's shoulder just as the red truck pulled nose-first into a vacant parking place three spaces down.

"You don't suppose he's coming here, do you?" Bernice said.

As if in answer, the truck door opened; out stepped a lone man in a big Stetson who could be no one but Linc Heller, and he headed in their direction.

All three women straightened in a hurry. The mayor's wife grabbed a bottle of the peaches from the display and suddenly became very interested in the hand-lettered label. And before Kansas knew what had hit her, Della had dragged her behind the counter where she'd been moments earlier and was handing her packages of cigarettes to stock in the rack alongside the cash register, a spot that blocked her vision of the door.

But Kansas knew the moment Linc Heller came in, because the bell sounded once more. And with it excitement rushed through her, even though she'd seen just enough to know her nephew wasn't with him.

Nothing much happened in the small town in which she'd grown up. The return of someone like Linc Heller felt akin to an event, no matter how much water had gone under the bridge since he'd last been home.

"Why, if it isn't Mrs. Watson," she heard him say when the door had closed behind him.

As he chatted amiably with the woman, Kansas eavesdropped unabashedly on the voice that was one of the deepest and richest she'd ever heard, a man's voice through and through, but with something very winning in it, as if it echoed a core-deep friendliness.

After a few moments he excused himself from Bernice, and the hollow, heavy clip of cowboy boots on the plank floor announced that he was headed for Kansas and Della.

Kansas was watching for him when he rounded the shelves that had blocked her view and it took only one look to tell her he was still one of the handsomest devils Elk Creek had ever produced. Better even than she remembered him as a younger man.

But after a split second's blank glance at her, his gaze went immediately to Della. "Delaware? Is that you?'' he asked, a small smile showing perfect white teeth and maybe just a hint of chagrin. But only a hint.

"Lincoln," Della greeted stiffly.

Kansas watched as his sparkling blue eyes took a quick assessment of her sister as if he had the right to, and then settled back on her face again. "How've you been?" he asked, as if he were genuinely pleased to see her.

"I'm just fine," Della informed him.

"That would have certainly been my guess," he said with a wry, appreciative little laugh that sounded admiring of the slightly plump physique that was the result of having given birth to four children.

Linc Heller had a way about him, Kansas realized both from what she'd overheard before and from this exchange now. He had the kind of deep-down, natural appeal that made even Della blush in a way that let Kansas know he'd scratched the surface of her sister's hard feelings toward him, even if only for a moment before Della drew herself up like a bird with ruffled feathers once more.

But Linc went on almost as if he saw that as a challenge. "Was old Bucky smart enough to hang on to you?"

"We're still married," she assured him.

"Kids?"

"Two boys and two girls."

He shook that handsome head. "Isn't that something. Well, it must suit you." Then his cornflower-blue gaze turned to Kansas and a frown drew a line between his thick eyebrows. It was clear that she looked familiar to him but that he wasn't sure who she was.

"Kansas," she offered.

Light dawned and made his mouth drop open for just a moment before he laughed. "Kansas? Little Kansas?"

"That's me. Well, except that I'm not little anymore," she said, hating the silly sound of it the moment she heard her own words.

But if he thought her foolish, it didn't show. One of those brows arched high, he cocked his head and gave her a thorough once-over. "You grew up real well, little Kansas."

It was on the tip of her tongue to say he had, too. Time had turned him into quite a man, sharpening the rugged planes of his face. Even the slight scar to the right of his strong forehead only added to his attractiveness.

His coffee-bean-colored hair was thick and just long enough to look rakish without being unkempt, though at the moment it was dented by a hat line that came from the big Stetson he'd been wearing when he'd gotten out of his truck. He had no doubt doffed it in deference to Bernice, because he carried it at his side now.

He had a brash nose that was long and pointed and just slightly flared around the nostrils; his jawline was strong and sharp. There was the same cocksure Heller dent in the center of his chin that marked both his father and his brother, and he had a mouth as supple as warm taffy, quick to smile in a way that seemed as if he was sharing a private joke with the recipient of it.

At that moment, he also had a cough that brought a big fist up to cover his mouth as he turned his head away from them.

For the first time Kansas realized he was wearing a leather jacket the same color as his eyes, with the collar turned up. Was it possible he was actually cold in the unseasonably warm eighty-five-degree heat?

"Are you sick?" Kansas asked.

"Caught some bug or another. That's why I came in—we need cough medicine, throat lozenges, baby aspirin—"

Kansas didn't hear anything after baby aspirin. She was too busy trying to think of a subtle way to ask about the nephew neither Linc nor her sister ever seemed to remember had any connection to anyone else.

"Danny..." she heard herself say. "That's his name, isn't it—your and Virgie's baby?"

"That's my boy, all right. He's under the weather, too, poor little guy."

"We have a doctor in town now, you know. If he needs one," Della offered in her mother's voice, showing signs that she was nowhere near as impervious to their nephew as she wanted Kansas to think she was.

"Neither of us is sick enough to need a doctor," Linc answered. "Just some rest and some aspirin."

"Don't you go giving that boy aspirin," Della went on in barely suppressed alarm. "Kids have to have the aspirin-free stuff."

Linc smiled indulgently, apparently not taking offense at Della's tone. "I know that, Delaware. I just call it aspirin out of habit. Now if one of you ladies would point me in the right direction—"

"I'll show you where it is," Kansas said then, rounding her sister and the counter to lead the way to the back of the store. "Is it just you and Danny at the ranch?" she asked along the way, fishing for information about a woman in his life.

"Just me and Danny," he confirmed. "I called Tilly next door to baby-sit while I came in here. Jackson is in Cheyenne on business."

"I'd heard Jackson was out of town," she muttered, feeling relieved to know there wasn't a woman traveling with them. "That's why I wondered if you had anyone to take care of you both . . . being sick the way you are." She was overcompensating for her nosiness and she knew it. She stopped before making it any worse.

"Danny and I'll be all right. We've been on our own for a long while now. . . ." This time it was Linc whose voice dwindled off, as if he'd realized too late to whom he was speaking and what that comment made reference to. And then he coughed again, racking his wide shoulders beneath the leather jacket and filling the tense silence that had sprung up between them.

They reached the medicine counter and he scanned the shelves, tapping his Stetson against the tight blue jeans that encased his thigh. "How're your folks doing?" he asked as he read labels.

"They're both well. They retired about five years ago and moved to Phoenix." Kansas paused a moment. "I'm sorry about your father."

"Thanks. But I hear he went quick. In the arms of a lady friend in Denver. Guess there are worse ways to go, especially when you're eighty." Then he said, "So, you and Della took over the store for your folks when they left?"

"Actually, I took it over. Della just comes in occasionally to help out when she can spare the time. But being the mother . . . of four kids keeps her pretty busy." Kansas hated the catch in her voice when she said the word *mother*. It was an involuntary reaction that had started when she'd had to accept the fact that she'd never be one.

She changed the subject in a hurry. "Do you have a thermometer?" she asked, taking one from where its packaging hung from a peg. "You need it if Danny might have a fever."

"Oh, we both have fevers, all right. He's hot to the touch, and the two of us are freezing one minute and sweatin' the next. I don't have to have one of those things to tell."

"You do, though," Kansas insisted, sounding slightly alarmed herself now. "Kids can get dangerously high fevers easier than adults and you might not know it without an exact reading of what his temperature is."

Linc smiled with only one side of his mouth and Kansas knew he thought she was overreacting. "Never had one before and we've done fine."

But Kansas knew she wouldn't be able to rest thinking that her nephew could be burning up and Linc wouldn't know it. She raised her chin to him and held out the thermometer. "Take it anyway—it's on the house—just to be sure."

For a moment he didn't reach for it. He didn't even look at it. Instead he seemed to study her, his expression part annoyance, part amusement. And as she met his gaze levelly, standing her ground, she couldn't help thinking that his eyes really were too beautiful to belong to a man.

Then his half smile turned into a knowing kind of grin. "Are you this much of a stickler about everything?"

She shrugged, feeling suddenly uncomfortable beneath his scrutiny. "Yes, I guess I am. I believe in doing things right."

"Every little thing, I'll bet."

He went on staring at her and somehow she knew he could tell simply by looking that she was an old-fashioned, follow-the-rules person who lived a quiet porch-sitting life. The exact opposite of what he was. Of what Virgie had been.

And for the first time in all of her twenty-nine years, Kansas wished she had some trick to pull out of a hat to prove it wasn't so and she could be just a little shocking.

But of course it was so.

Linc finally took the thermometer, turned back to the shelf and went on looking for what he needed. "Are you married, Kansas? Have kids?"

She took a deep breath and slipped her hands protectively into her pockets. "No."

"Married and divorced, or never married?"

"Never."

"Couldn't do it right, so you didn't do it at all, is that it?" he teased with such good-natured aplomb that it wasn't insulting.

It was, however, true. Basically. But she didn't say that. She said, "I just never married," as if it hadn't been all tied up with what she considered the worst thing to have ever happened to her.

"Hmm. Must be a lot of blind men in this town," he murmured as he finally began to gather what he'd decided to buy. And Kansas gained an understanding of what Della had felt in response to his compliment.

"I suppose this should take care of us," he said when he'd chosen a broad spectrum of remedies and used his upturned hat as a shopping basket to hold everything. "Unless I've missed something," he added, looking at Kansas out of the corner of eyes that seemed still amused by her.

"Come on up to the front," was all she said in answer, leading the way back to the cash register that Della had abandoned in order to help Bernice.

"So. Are you back just for the time being or to stay?" Kansas asked as she rang up his merchandise.

"A little of both," he answered without really answering at all. And he seemed to have no inclination to make himself clearer.

"I hear Beth is coming home, too," Kansas said, to fill the silence.

"Any time now. She and Jackson and I have to sort through things."

"I'll be glad to see her again."

"Mmm-hmm."

"Has she ever met Danny?" Kansas asked in a tone that was too subtle to be subtle at all and made her want to kick herself.

"Never has, no."

She arrived at a total and told him what it was, watching as he reached into his back pocket for his wallet. And then, somehow, her glance fell to his waist, where a four-inch silver belt buckle rode just above his zipper.

Surprised at herself, she quickly averted her eyes.

He paid for his purchases, but once Kansas had put the medicines in a bag for him, she felt a sharp tug of reluctance to hand it over and have him leave. At least before she'd made some headway over her nephew.

But even though she didn't know if it was warranted, she felt the same way she might have around a skittish horse—that one false move might send Linc off in the opposite direction and cost her what she wanted most.

She cleared her throat and ventured forth as if walking on eggs. "You know, we've never met Danny, either, and we'd really like to."

His response was to chuckle maddeningly. "Course you would. Soon as he's feeling better I'll bring him around."

A bubble of relief floated up in Kansas and made her forgive him for laughing at her. "Oh, good," she breathed, raising a smile his way only to find him staring at her again, this time so intently she almost felt heat emanating from his eyes.

"Danny looks like you," he said then. "I didn't realize it until now. His hair is more your color than that lighter brown of Della's and Virgie's. And he has your eyes, too, green as grapes and shot through with those darker streaks. I've wondered who it was he looked like all this time."

It gave Kansas's heart another little tug to think of the nephew she'd never seen and the similarities between them. Or maybe a part of what tugged at her heart was Linc himself, sort of a flashback to that old adolescent crush she'd had on the boy who had the talent for making everyone feel special.

She shook herself out of her reverie. "Anytime," she said with that hated catch in her voice again. "We'd love to meet him anytime at all. And if you need something—with Jackson being gone and you feeling sick—just call."

He smiled at her, all the teasing gone from his expression. "I'll do that." Then he cocked his head and chuckled. "Yes, sir, little Kansas definitely did grow up." And he took his bag and headed for the door.

But before he reached it, he stopped at the end of the aisle where Della was helping Bernice. "Be seeing you both. Della, tell old Bucky I'm going to look him up. And Mrs. Watson, you give the mayor my best."

Then he left and Kansas watched him as he back-tracked to his truck, tossing her another smile and a small wave when he caught her at it. But still she went right on looking until she saw that cocky red truck pass by and disappear around the corner.

"Kansas? Kansas?" Della's voice drew her attention to the fact that the other two women had re-joined her without her noticing it. "Do you have more of those sweet pickles the mayor likes? I can't find any on the shelves."

It took a moment for her to concentrate. "No, I'm sorry, but we're sold out. Sarah Simms is putting up a new batch, though. They should be in early next week."

While Bernice and Della discussed the merits and demerits of Sarah Simms's canning methods, Kansas totaled the older woman's groceries and magazines and took the money for them.

It was only as she put everything in sacks that she discovered the thermometer she'd set aside so as not to charge Linc for it.

"Oh, no," she muttered to herself, worried all over again that her nephew might be spiking a fever higher than his laid-back father realized.

It was nearly closing time and she knew Della would head home in the general direction of the ranch. She could ask her to take it out to Linc.

But Della had a baby-sitter to let go, and supper to fix, and she was already doing Kansas a favor by coming in to help unload the day's delivery. Kansas hated to ask more of her.

Then, too, if she did it herself, she'd have the chance to meet Danny after all.

Kansas slipped the thermometer into the breast pocket of her shirt alongside her glasses, certain that the little boy was the only reason the idea of driving out to the Heller place seemed so appealing, that it didn't have anything to do with Linc.

Yet when she'd said goodbye to the mayor's wife and sent Della on her way, she went into the bathroom off the storage room in the back of the store and brushed a few swipes of blush onto her cheekbones.

But that didn't have anything to do with Linc Heller, either, she swore to herself. It was just a matter of freshening up a little at the end of the day.

And the only reason her heart was beating double time was because going out to the ranch meant she would finally get to see her nephew.

Chapter Two

Linc felt like something the cat wouldn't bother to drag in as he turned off the light in the bedroom his son was using at the ranch. He'd given Danny the pain reliever and a bath to cool the little boy's fever. The combination of the two had made Danny nearly asleep on his feet as Linc dried him off, so he'd put him down for a nap.

Now it was Linc's turn.

His head hurt, his muscles hurt, his skin hurt, even his hair hurt. He'd taken bad falls from the wildest bucking broncos that hadn't left him feeling this bad. He hadn't even felt this rotten after the car accident. Not physically, anyway.

Or maybe he had and he just didn't remember it, the way he didn't remember a lot about the time after he'd regained consciousness from that three-week coma. He had a vivid memory of being told that Virgie was dead, that she'd already been sent back home for burial, but for a month or so from there things were blurry.

But he didn't want to think about that.

As he went into the living room he undid his belt buckle and the button on the waistband of his jeans to get comfortable. Then he retrieved the remote control from the top of the big-screen television and took it with him to one of the three couches that formed a U around it.

From there he turned on the TV and then he pulled off his boots—silver-gray snakeskin from a company he'd just signed on with to endorse their clothes and footwear, a perk left over from taking a world champion title at the National Finals Rodeo in Las Vegas the December before.

One by one the heavy shoes hit the floor, followed by his socks, and then he stretched out on the sofa, using the armrest as a pillow and wielding the remote as he waited for the aspirin he'd taken to kick in.

The evening news was on most channels. He flipped through them until he found an old sitcom—three fresh-faced sisters bickering over who was going to a dance with a boy they were all staking claim to. It made him think of the Daye sisters a long time ago.

Delaware, Virginia and Kansas.

Their father had spent his childhood in several states as a military brat, but those three had been his favorites and so he'd christened his daughters with their names.

Della, the oldest, had been the cantankerous one. No change there, Linc thought wryly. Though a little sweet talk still seemed to help.

Then there'd been Virgie, the middle child. The wild one. Prettier than Della; louder and more outrageous by far, wanting to try any forbidden fruit, push every limit, every boundary. Reckless and hell-bent . . .

Like him.

To a point.

The point where he'd grown up and she hadn't.

And then there was Kansas.

Little Kansas . . .

She had been a twelve-year-old kid the last time Linc saw her, at Della's wedding, the day before he and Virgie had run off to follow the rodeo circuit.

He'd missed seeing her when he'd come back to help Jackson with the ranch later on because she'd been away at college. And now nearly another eight years had passed.

No wonder he hadn't recognized her. The last time he'd seen Kansas Daye she hadn't come into her own as a girl yet.

It made him smile to remember her as the tomboy she'd been then, with her hair cut nearly as short as a man's and her scrawny flat-chested body.

Her face hadn't changed a whole lot, though, he realized, just matured, filled out. She'd always been pretty—softer featured than Virgie. Even all those years ago she'd had that nose that turned up just a tad at the end, and those pale lips, and that slightly pointy chin that she poked out insistently when her strong will was showing—like today over that thermometer.

Where was that thing, anyway?

He felt too rotten to care and instead slipped back to thinking about Kansas. In his mind, he had a vivid picture of her, and he closed his eyes to savor the image.

Long hair suited her, though he'd have rather seen the shiny, coppery-brown silk falling free, more the way her swept-over bangs were.

She was still just a little bit of a woman but she wasn't flat-chested anymore. At least from what he could tell through the shirt that hid most everything. She seemed proportioned the way a woman ought to be—enough to hold on to, just a handful everywhere....

Not that he intended to find out.

She'd gone from tomboy to straitlaced woman, if he was any judge. And he was.

All buttoned up and hiding behind her clothes, worrying about the exact numbers to tell if a boy had a fever when Linc had already told her he could feel it for himself; she'd been wearing tennis shoes she'd polished, for pity's sake! And she was all careful to tiptoe around how she wanted to see Danny, instead of just asking when the hell he was going to let the boy know he had family that was chomping at the bit to meet him, and giving Linc the dressing-down he deserved for not having brought the boy back long ago.

But she did have the damned most beautiful eyes he'd ever seen. And lashes long enough to sweep stalls. She smelled like something straight from heaven. And she had a behind built for a man's hand....

Damn it all to hell, he didn't need to be thinking about that, either.

He opened his eyes to watch television again.

That was when he noticed Danny standing there. His son was staring at him with a solemn expression that looked so much like the one Linc's brother, Jackson, wore most of the time that there was no doubting they were related. Danny just stood there, waiting and watching, sucking his thumb, with his index finger inside one corner of the satin edging of his raggedy old blanket, stroking the tip of his nose at the same time. It had been a short nap.

"Feeling any better, little guy?"

Danny just shook his head, taking his thumb along for the ride.

"Want to lie with me?"

This time the boy's head went up and down.

Linc held out his arms and Danny climbed on top of him, his small head on Linc's chest just below Linc's chin, with his legs on either side of Linc's stomach, as if he were on horseback, and his thumb and blanket corner back in his mouth the moment he was settled.

Linc spread the rest of the blanket to cover the boy before curving an arm over him. Then he picked up the remote control again with his other hand.

"Let's see if this fancy satellite dish your ol' Uncle Jackson has here can bring in some cartoons."

One by one he flipped through the stations, passing political talk shows, home shopping, a black-and-white movie.

And then he hit a country network and paused.

"Tha's you," Danny said with a slight adjustment of his thumb.

"That's me, all right," Linc confirmed as they both watched the airing of the rodeo competition he'd ridden in a few weeks before.

Even judging what he saw with a critical eye, he was proud of it. He'd stayed on the bronc's back the full eight seconds until the buzzer sounded, and his form had been right on the mark.

Listening to the flattering commentary and seeing the excitement he'd generated gave him a deep feeling of satisfaction. But there was no rush like a good ride. And that twenty-five-thousand-dollar purse had paid off the last of the medical bills with some cash left over.

Funny how things worked out. Just when he'd gotten himself out of debt, he inherited a quarter share of a sizable estate that would easily have paid for the accident and let him set up a home base for Danny instead of dragging him around the whole country since then.

"I wanna see cart-toons," Danny ordered, pulling Linc out of his reverie.

"I don't know if there are any on," Linc said, but he started running through the channels again to see, thinking about being back in Elk Creek for good this time as he did. Back where he'd grown up and raised hell and fallen in love with Virgie.

Seemed like two lifetimes ago.

Virgie was gone. His father was gone. The ranch belonged to Jackson, for all intents and purposes, regardless of the fact that Linc and Beth were part owners on paper. Virgie's folks were retired and moved on. Della was a mother of four. And Kansas was a grown woman...

He finally found cartoons for Danny and set down the remote. But what was on the television screen didn't interest him and his thoughts wandered once more to the Dayes.

On the way back to Elk Creek he'd wondered how Virgie's family would respond to him this time around. During his last visit here, they'd been barely civil, and that was before Virgie's death. Things might have changed for the worse since then, and he'd figured the best he could hope for was more of the same.

That's about what he'd gotten from Della. But Kansas had been another story. She'd been formal but friendly, and that had been a nice surprise. A real nice surprise.

Of course it could be she was interested only in Danny, he told himself.

But that was okay. Because it was for Danny's sake that Linc had come back to Elk Creek.

And yet, as he rubbed his son's back and saw again in his mind's eye the image of Kansas, he couldn't keep himself from hoping that it wasn't only Danny who would be in line for more of the warmth in those beautiful green eyes.

Kansas almost forgot to lock the store's back door as she went out that way to her tan station wagon parked in the alley. She opened the passenger door and set a sack of oranges on the seat to take to Linc and Danny, adding the thermometer from her shirt pocket while she was at it, and thinking about how long it had been since she'd gone to the Heller ranch.

She'd spent a considerable amount of time there as a girl, because she and Beth—the youngest Heller and the only daughter—had been good friends.

But they'd gone away to different colleges after high school, and when that was finished, Kansas had come back to Elk Creek while Beth had married and gone to live with her husband on the Wind River Indian Reservation in Fort Washakie.

Over the years, Beth hadn't returned, so Kansas hadn't had any reason to go the ranch. She'd thought, when Shag Heller died, that she'd get to see her old friend at the funeral, but he'd died in Denver and for some reason no one understood, he'd been buried there. That had disappointed two of Kansas's hopes—that she'd see Beth and that she'd get to meet her nephew, too.

Now she rounded the car, got in behind the wheel and, once she had the engine started, left a cloud of dust in her hurry to finally do the second of those two things.

Kansas was crazy about all of her nieces and nephews, so being anxious to know Danny wasn't out of the ordinary for her. She loved kids and had always just assumed she'd have a lot of her own.

But some twists of fate were particularly unkind and she knew, now, that she never would.

She didn't like to dwell on that, though. She'd learned in the past year that it didn't help to feel sorry for herself.

Besides, she had Della's kids to spoil. And now Danny, too.

The sun was still high as she rounded the block onto Center Street. Kansas pushed the button on the main control panel and lowered only the rear car windows so as not to get windblown. But even with the front ones still up, in came the rich scents of freshly mowed grass, flowers in full bloom and steaks being sizzled for the dinner crowd at one of Elk Creek's two restaurants.

Most everything was closed for the day as she headed north on the street that bisected the small town—hence its name. Stately old buildings, quaint and charactered, stood on either side. One, two, three storied. Some flat-faced and stern; others spired and ornate; a few that were nondescript but dressed up with shutters on either side of paned windows, looking like cottages; all housing offices and stores that saw to just about every need any of Elk Creek's citizens had.

The cross streets held a few also-ran shops before melting into the homes of townsfolk and turning into a maze of avenues where houses cropped up, some of identical design, others the heart's delight of their owners, but all modest and lovingly tended, and many passed down from parents to children or grandchildren.

At the far north end of Center Street was the courthouse, an imposing redbrick structure with a clock tower that rivaled the church next door's steeple. The old Molner mansion on the other side had been remodeled into a medical facility, and the three buildings together curved around the park square, where oak trees formed a canopy for the festivals, bazaars and town picnics that brought everyone together periodically.

And rarely did Kansas pass it all without feeling as if this were the one place on earth that she was meant to live.

Elk Creek, Wyoming.

To her, it was the perfect spot to grow up, marry, raise children and while away later years watching the cycle renew itself. And even if the children weren't her own, it was a place where everyone knew everyone and, for the most part, wished them well, sharing the pleasure of their triumphs, the pain of their tragedies, and the day-to-day ups and downs in between, much like a great big family, all connected and caring even if there was a little bickering every now and then.

Kansas was glad that Linc had chosen to bring Danny back here. She only hoped he meant to stay.

On her way out of town, she passed the school, where small children were putting the new playground equipment to good use while their parents rooted for their older brothers at the baseball field on the other side.

Beyond that was the sheriff's office and, slightly farther out, the Heller's lumber mill. But all of it—from the south end of Elk Creek where the train station started the town proper, to here—could be walked in half an hour.

As she drove by the mill, Rick Meyers was just coming out, probably the last to leave, since he was the foreman. Kansas waved at him and he waved back, calling hello as he did.

After that, though, only flat, open, Heller-owned cornfields led the way to the ranch house.

Heller property went on for the next thousand acres north and all the way east to the Nebraska state line. Shag's grandfather had been one of the two founders of Elk Creek, staking a claim to a good portion of the current holdings right from the start. Each subsequent generation had added to it until half of the town itself and its surrounding area was in the Heller name.

Now, it all belonged to Jackson, Beth and Linc. And, rumor had it, to old Shag's lady friend in Denver, but that hadn't been confirmed.

The house wasn't far from town and came into Kansas's sight within ten minutes of the lumber mill.

Built like a mountain cabin, its split log walls were held together by mortar. A two-storied H-shaped structure, it stretched out like a lazy dog in the sunshine, taking up enough space to build two city houses with big yards in between.

Kansas drove halfway into the circular driveway that wrapped around a plain patch of flawless lawn, and stopped the car directly in front of the house, behind Linc's outlandish red truck.

Shag Heller had not been a fancy man, so there were no flower beds to decorate the grounds and nothing but a cobbled floor in the whole of the center courtyard.

Since her earlier days out here with Beth, Kansas knew a heliport had been added somewhere far enough away from the stables behind the house not to spook the horses. But other than that, the place looked the same—stately but rustic.

Kansas took the grocery bag and got out of the car. It occurred to her for the first time then that Linc might not appreciate her visit. He'd obviously thought the thermometer unnecessary from the start, and even though Kansas had made it clear that she wanted to meet Danny, Linc hadn't extended an invitation for her to do that today; he'd only said he would bring the boy around sometime.

But there she was, standing on the gravel driveway, and she wasn't about to turn back now.

She blew her bangs out of her eyes, squared her shoulders and headed for the house.

Deep inside the courtyard, she rang the doorbell, but rather than the big, rough-hewn panel being opened, she heard Linc's voice from inside say, "Come on in."

It wasn't unusual in Elk Creek for doors to be left unlocked, but still Kansas wondered if he was expecting company. Nevertheless, she turned the handle and stepped into the cool, dim foyer.

It took her eyes a moment to adjust from the bright sunlight outside to the nearly dark interior of the house. While they did, she just stood there on the slate-tiled floor, trying to focus on the huge coat tree standing against the left wall and the round pedestal table that took up the center.

When she could see again, she looked beyond the table to the living room, which dropped down three steps below and sprawled like a castle's wide-open great room. But it was still hard to see. The drapes were all pulled, the walls were certainly too thick to bleed light, and the only electric illumination came from the big-screen television that faced the foyer at a long distance away on the wall at the opposite side of the H's center.

"Linc?" she called tentatively when no one appeared. "It's Kansas."

A long arm went up from the overstuffed sofa with its back to the entranceway. "We're down here," his deep, resonant voice answered, as casually as if he'd been waiting for her.

Her tennis shoes were silent on the slate floor as she crossed it, and when she descended the steps to the sunken living room, she found herself in thick-piled carpet. She rounded the couch and discovered Linc lying on his back with a tiny, blanket-covered body lying over him like a jungle boy dangling his arms and legs over a tree branch.

"I forgot to give you the thermometer," she said by way of explaining why she was there, stopping at the foot of the sofa. "And I brought some oranges. I thought maybe the juice would taste good to you both.''

"You didn't have to do that."

"I wanted to. It's no trouble."

"I'd get up, but I think he's sleeping," Linc said, pointing a finger at the mound under the blanket.

"That's okay," she assured him, but she couldn't keep her distance from her nephew another minute. Kansas slipped between the big square coffee table and the sofa Linc was lying on, squatting down on her haunches while she still hugged the grocery bag to her chest. "This is Danny?" she asked in a bare whisper, even though Linc had been using a normal voice.

"The one and only," he answered.

With a single index finger, Kansas carefully moved the blanket just enough to see the boy's face. Long, sooty eyelashes dusted round cheeks, and his small pink mouth sucked furiously on his chubby thumb. "Oh, he's so beautiful."

"Handsome, maybe, but don't go calling my son beautiful and making a sissy out of him."

Kansas couldn't tell if Linc was teasing, but being acutely aware of the fact that she'd come here uninvited, and that she was an in-law, she didn't assume he was. "Handsome," she amended somewhat primly, wishing she could scoop the child up into her arms and hold him on her lap. Instead, she sat back on her heels and hazarded a glance at Linc.

He was watching her intently from beneath a frown that pulled his full brows together over the bridge of his nose.

Kansas rushed on. "I'm sorry, I know you're not feeling up to company and you said you'd bring Danny around, but I wanted so badly to see him.

Forgetting the thermometer really was an accident, but there it was and I just thought, well, why don't I bring it out, and—"

"What are you apologizing for, Kansas?" he asked in part exasperation, part amusement. "Look at you there, holding that sack like a schoolgirl using her books as a shield. I don't bite and I didn't say you weren't welcome, did I?"

"No, but—"

"Then quit pussyfootin' around me. I appreciate that you want to see Danny and that you're thinking about what we might need out here. Hell, I'm glad to see you. So relax."

Kansas had remembered what a sweet-talker he was. But she hadn't remembered how blunt he could be, too. Still, she was happy to know she wasn't trespassing.

"Who're you?" a sleepy little voice said, drawing Linc's chin downward and Kansas's gaze to the bundle that hadn't moved so much as a hair except to open wide, pale green eyes.

One look into them and Kansas fell in love. "I'm Kansas," she said, wanting to declare herself his aunt but thinking he might not understand.

"Remember how we talked about the people you'd see when we came here?" Linc asked, speaking into the tousled head of auburn waves. "Remember I told you there would be aunts and uncles? Well, this is one of your aunts."

Danny seemed to take that at face value, showing neither confusion nor any particular interest, but only solemn acceptance.

So solemn that it made Kansas smile and glance at Linc. "Is he always this serious or is it just that he's sick?"

"He's always this serious. Like—"

"Jackson," Kansas finished for him, winning a slight chuckle and a nod of Linc's handsome head.

Sitting down on the floor the way she was, she was not only very near her nephew, but Linc, as well. Too close not to notice the dark stubble of his beard that was beginning to show, the deep hollows of his cheeks, the rawboned beauty of his profile. Not to mention the wide span of his chest and shoulders, which made a more than adequate bed for his son.

Danny pushed himself to a sitting position, still straddling his father's stomach and saving Kansas from her own thoughts. "Wha's in there?" he asked, pointing to the bag she held.

She wished she had something more fun than oranges and a thermometer to show him, but since that was all there was, it was the only answer she could give. "Do you like orange juice?" she asked when she'd shown him the contents.

He looked to Linc. "Do I?"

"Yes, you do," Linc answered, keeping his big hands on either side of the child's hips even though Danny didn't seem to need bracing.

"Yep, I do," the little boy repeated to Kansas as if she hadn't heard his father.

"How about if we take your temperature first and then I'll squeeze you and your daddy some juice?"

"No," Danny decreed flatly.

"He won't be three for a few days yet, Kansas. That means he's still in the terrible twos. *No* is his favorite word. I'm hoping that'll change sometime soon after his birthday." Lifting his son, Linc sat up, swung his feet to the floor and then replaced the boy on his lap. "Your Aunt Kansas is going to take your temperature so she can feel better," he said with a wry glance her way.

"I'm a'ready bedder. I wan' juice."

Linc nodded to the space on the sofa he'd just vacated. "Sit up here, Kansas, and I'll get you an armpit," he said, ignoring Danny's protest as he unsnapped his son's pajamas.

Kansas was surprised he knew to take the child's temperature under his arm. But she forgot about it a moment later when she slipped up to the couch and the warmth left from Linc's body wrapped around her. Then she started wondering why a thing like that should make her pulse pick up speed.

Danny lay limply against Linc's black T-shirted chest and let Kansas put the thermometer under his arm. He scowled at her but didn't make a fuss.

Once it was in place, she gently held his tiny arm against his body to hold it there.

He was warm enough for it to be evident he had a fever just from the feel of his skin, but not warm enough to be alarming. Linc had been right, she realized, and along with that came the sudden knowledge that she'd just assumed he wouldn't be a conscientious, responsible father.

But he was.

Whatever else Linc Heller might be—hell-raiser, rambler, reckless rodeo cowboy—he was a good father. With or without a thermometer. He seemed to be as naturally talented at that as he was at everything else.

"Have you guys eaten?" Kansas asked, glancing from her nephew to Linc.

"Not yet. How about you?"

"I came straight from the store. If you're hungry, I'll fix something for you before I go."

Linc's agile mouth quirked up on just one side. "Doesn't take much to open a can of soup or microwave a frozen dinner. We'd be happy for your company, though, if you'd like to stay and eat with us."

"I wan' cereal," Danny informed them.

Kansas cast the boy a smile before glancing back at Linc. "I'm on my way to a potluck dinner at the church, but thanks for the invitation."

"Anytime."

She realized Linc looked a little ragged around the edges, but even at that, he was still a feast for the eyes, and Kansas found it surprisingly difficult not to indulge.

It helped when the thermometer beeped to let her know the temperature had registered.

She slipped it out from under her nephew's arm and read it. "You were right—he has a fever, but nothing serious."

Linc poked his strong, dented chin her way. "Does that put your mind to rest?"

"Yes." That, and seeing how good Linc was with the boy. Now if only other things inside her would rest and she could stop noticing details like his hair teasing the tops of his ears; the thickness of his neck ringed by the crew collar of his T-shirt; the width of his arms where his biceps stretched the short sleeves ...

Kansas took a deep breath and fought the thoughts.

She replaced the cover on the thermometer, set it on the coffee table and picked up the bag of oranges.

"I'm going to go into the kitchen to squeeze some juice, so why don't you let me fix your supper while I'm there, and then I'll get going?"

"You really are hell-bent on feeding us, aren't you?"

She was actually more hell-bent on putting some distance between herself and Linc without having to leave just yet. "I want to get you both well so I can spend some time with my nephew," she said in a way that sounded much more stuffy and supercilious than she meant it to. She hoped it hadn't seemed that way to him.

She stood and for a moment Linc stared up at her with another of those amused smiles of his. Then he said to Danny, "I'm going to leave you here to watch these 'toons while I show your Aunt Kansas where the kitchen is."

"I know where it is," she said quickly. "When Beth and I were in high school we got to be good friends, and I spent a lot of time out here."

But Linc sat Danny on the couch beside him and got up anyway, pecking what seemed like an unconscious kiss on the boy's head as if it were something he always did. Then he shot Kansas a glance and nodded toward the floor. "Don't trip over my boots."

Kansas had noticed them before. Just as she'd noticed his big bare feet with their blunt toes, nearly nonexistent arch, the pink, healthy look they had, and how strangely intimate it seemed to be in their company...

He stepped over the boots and she followed, trailing her gaze up from where it had somehow gotten back on those naked feet of his. His jean-encased legs were long, thickly muscled enough to hang on to a bucking horse, and bowed slightly. And above them was a tight derriere that fit into his two back pockets like a charm.

He wore his jeans slung slightly low, but certainly not out of necessity the way some men did to accommodate big bellies. No, his belly couldn't have been flatter or his waist narrower, or his shoulders broader, or...

Kansas yanked her gaze away from him as they made their way through the dining room, around the long oak table that would easily seat thirty, and went through a swinging door into the kitchen.

Linc flipped a switch and bright, recessed light flooded a room nearly as big as Kansas's whole house and well equipped enough to belong to a small restaurant. There was a commercial-size refrigerator, an eight-burner stainless steel stove with two ovens, a dishwasher, two pantries, cupboards galore and a central butcher block that could support a whole side of beef without any problem.

Like the rest of the Heller place, it was more functional than fashionable, and yet there was a warmth to it in the navy blue tiled walls and countertops and the crisp white cupboards.

"I'd forgotten the size of this kitchen," Kansas said when they were in the middle of it.

"I'll do you one better than that—I'd forgotten how big the whole place is," Linc said. "Makes me feel like I have full run of a hotel."

"You don't like it?" she asked, interpreting his tone and surprised by it.

He shrugged and her eyes rode along atop the squarest shoulder she'd ever seen. "I like a cozier place," he said.

"The Shea house is up for sale next door to me," she heard herself say, though the words came out even as she debated about the wisdom of the idea. She'd have liked nothing better than to have Danny settled in a few feet from her house. But having Linc that nearby suddenly seemed a little dangerous.

"You're not living in your folks' old house?" he asked rather than comment on what she'd said.

"Della's family is there. I didn't need all those rooms. I bought the O'Donnell's house on First Street when Mrs. O'Donnell died and Shelline didn't want it."

Linc nodded slowly. He'd leaned his hips back against the counter and crossed his arms over his chest.

She hadn't noticed before that his belt and his waistband button were undone. He'd probably unfastened them when he'd lain on the couch, not expecting company, and forgotten about it. Nothing showed. But there was that big, shiny buckle dangling down beside his zipper and for some reason, the sight of it made Kansas's mouth go dry.

She turned swiftly to the cupboard where pitchers had been kept years ago. They still were, so she took one down. Then she busied herself washing oranges and rolling them on the countertop to soften them.

As she worked, she could feel those piercing eyes of his watching her. It only added to how unnerved she already was in view of her oddly heightened awareness of him.

"We'd all about given up any thought that you'd ever come back," she said out of the blue. The words had come on their own, and once they were out she realized she probably shouldn't have said them.

Yet he didn't hesitate to answer, seeming undisturbed. "I imagine so."

"Did you stay away on purpose or was it just something that happened?"

"Both. It's easy to lose track of time when there's always another rodeo in another city, another try at winnings that'll not only pay the bills but add up to get you into the finals in Vegas. And when you're not actually rodeoing or getting ready to, you're traveling to the next one."

"Then that's how it just happened that you stayed away. How was it on purpose?" she persisted when he seemed to stall, thinking that she'd come this far, she might as well go all the way, and feeling emboldened by not having to look at him directly as she cut the oranges.

But this time he didn't answer as readily. Only after a moment did he say, "Ah, Kansas, you know."

She glanced out of the corner of her eye, finding him staring up at the ceiling, his thick neck arched, his Adam's apple poked out, all masculine and sexy...

Kansas swallowed hard and tried to reign in even her peripheral vision.

Then he went on. "The idea of coming back here was hard to warm up to after the way Virgie and I left. Your folks and Virgie ended up with a lot of bad blood between them. And my father...well, Shag was never an easy one to get along with, and he and I weren't on the best of terms. He thought ridin' rodeo was a worthless, shiftless life and made sure I knew it. Said if I didn't kill myself, I'd come running home with my tail between my legs, begging him to take me in."

"But you did come back for a while."

"Only for Jackson's sake—to help him—and because Shag wasn't around. Then Shag showed up, we fought all over again and just when I'd started to think it might be nice to visit now and then if I could talk your sister into it, he made me not want to ever come back."

"But here you are now," she reminded.

He shoved away from the counter and went to one of the pantries for cereal. "Here I am, all right."

"But only because your father's gone?"

He laughed in a way that sounded as if he were laughing at himself. "No, as a matter of fact I was aiming for Elk Creek when Jackson tracked me down to tell me Shag had passed on."

"For a visit?" she asked, still working on the oranges.

He came to stand near her to get a bowl down from the cupboard and as he reached for it she could feel the heat emanating from him. Was he still feverish? she wondered. Or was she just that sensitive to him?

Once he had the bowl he stayed put, leaning a hip against the drawer beside her. "More than a visit. The truth is, I wanted to come back to Elk Creek when Danny was born."

Kansas's eyes went to him on their own. "You did?"

He chucked her gently under the chin with a curved forefinger. "Don't look so shocked."

"But then why didn't you?"

"That's another long story I don't think I'm up to telling you right now."

Silence fell between them for a moment until Kansas had to break it. "Does that mean you're staying, then?"

"I'm setting up a home base for Danny and me."
He looked around the kitchen. "But it won't be in this
house."

Somehow *setting up a home base* didn't sound as if
he were really settling down for good. "Are you giving up rodeoing?"

"Not till I'm too old or broken up to hold on," he
answered as if she were out of her mind.

"But—"

He stopped her from saying more with a barrel-deep
chuckle and the tip of his index finger pressed to her
lips. "We're going to have plenty of time to talk about
all this. But right now if I don't get off these aching
bones I'm going to fall on my face."

His finger against her mouth was hot, his eyes
sparkled down into hers, and Kansas's mind went
completely blank.

Then he took his finger away and reached up for a
second bowl. "Cornflakes sounds pretty good to me,
too. Think I'll stick with it myself."

That brought Kansas back to her senses. "Neither
of you should eat just cereal for supper. Let me fix you
something else."

"Cereal is all we want, Kansas. Cereal and that juice
you squeezed. Haven't had fresh OJ since I was a
kid." And that said, he poured milk and cornflakes
into the bowls, picked them up and shouldered
through the swinging door to get out of the kitchen.

Kansas watched him go, tall and lean and powerful
looking, and swaggering just a little the way he did
when he walked. She thought that it was hard to look
at him and remember he was sick. But he was. And
now wasn't the time to ask him all the things she was
curious about.

She cleaned the countertop, rounded up two glasses and took them along with the pitcher into the living room, where Danny sat on the floor between the sofa and the table with his face close to the bowl in front of him and milk on his chin. Linc sat on the coffee table itself, his bowl beside him as if he weren't going to eat after all.

"Sure you don't want to join us?" he asked wryly, nodding at the breakfast food.

She poured the juice and set a glass near each of their bowls. "No, really. I need to go. But I'd like to come back tomorrow, if that would be okay. Maybe bring you some soup? You do like soup, don't you? Or I could make whatever sounds good to you or—"

Before she even realized she was within his reach, she found her hand clasped in Linc's big, callused one.

"You're pussyfootin' around again, Kansas. What'd I tell you about that?"

This time she laughed. "Okay. Tomorrow I'll make soup and bring it by for supper so you eat something more substantial than cornflakes. Whether you like it or not," she added forcefully.

"That's better," he judged, squeezing her hand.

But he didn't let go. Instead, he rubbed the back of it with light circular strokes of his thumb, sending a skitter of goose bumps up her arm.

"Thanks for coming out here," he said then. "If I was in better shape I'd show you just how much I appreciate it."

"I'll bet you would," she countered, surprised at herself and how glib she sounded, almost flirtatious, which was unlike her.

And then, when he released her hand, she felt a wave of disappointment at losing his touch and was even more shocked at her own reaction.

She escaped it with renewed interest in Danny, reminding herself that her nephew was her real reason for being here.

Kansas went to the other side of the table and again squatted down to be at eye level with the boy. "I hope you feel better, Danny. I'll see you tomorrow and maybe bring you some ice cream—would you like that?"

"Shocolate," he informed her solemnly.

"Chocolate," she assured. "Is there anything else you're hungry for?"

"Suckers and snow cones and shocolate candy bars."

Kansas smiled but glanced to Linc before promising anything else. It was no surprise to find his blue eyes on her again, because she'd sensed he was watching her once more, though she didn't understand why.

"The ice cream will be plenty," he said.

Kansas nodded and then turned her attention back to Danny, venturing to move a strand of wavy hair off his forehead with just an index finger. "I'll see you tomorrow," she repeated.

"Bye," the little boy answered as he crawled onto the sofa again, retrieved his blanket and cuddled up with a corner of it and his thumb in his mouth to watch the cartoons that still played on the television.

Kansas couldn't resist rubbing his tiny back just a little. By the time she tore herself away, Linc was on his feet to walk her to the door.

"Don't get up. I'll let myself out."

But just as he'd ignored her attempt not to have him go with her into the kitchen, he ignored this and followed her to the entranceway.

"Like I said, if you need anything, don't hesitate to call," she repeated as she opened the door. But before she could step outside, she had to glance one last time in Danny's direction. "He seems like a good boy. Thanks for letting me see him."

One of Linc's big hands cupped her chin and turned her to face him. His head was shaking—a slow back-and-forth motion—and his mouth was barely curved up on one side in a wry smile that seemed to say he thought she was hopeless about pussyfooting around him.

"You can see Danny whenever you want, Kansas. He needs to get to know his family."

"Good," she answered, putting some muscle into the word. "It's about time."

That made him laugh. And then, catching her completely off guard, he kissed her forehead. A simple kiss that kept his warm lips pressed to her skin for a moment longer than he might have and sent a flood of very confusing emotions through her.

"Thanks for coming," he said when he'd let her go.

Kansas was a little slow on the uptake. "Sure," she managed finally, stepping out into the warmth of the sun, which was lower in the sky by then. "Good night."

He tapped a single index finger to his temple and then pointed it her way. "Tomorrow," he said, with a lifting of his chin and a tone of voice that sounded as if he were looking forward to it.

Kansas went to her car then, but once she was behind the wheel she glanced back at the house.

Linc was still standing in the open doorway, his back against the jamb, one hand hidden under the opposite arm, the other poked into his jean pocket, and a devilish quirk to his lips.

Kansas answered with a quivery smile of her own as she started the engine and pulled the rest of the way around the circular driveway.

But even as she left, she kept him in sight in her rearview mirror. All the while wondering what on earth had gotten into her.

And why he kept standing there, watching her go.

Chapter Three

Not a day went by that Kansas didn't look at the scar.

Every morning she stepped out of the tub facing the full-length mirror on the back of the door and there it was.

Some days she could make herself turn away from the sight, but other days she felt compelled to study it. Today was one of those days.

A smile just below the bikini line.

That was what the doctor had promised. As if swim wear had mattered to her at that moment.

The scar was still a bright pink color, but it wasn't angry-looking anymore, and by now it was healed so completely that it barely tingled when she ran her fingertips over it.

But behind the scar she felt an emptiness. A deep, gaping emptiness.

That was silly, she knew. The actual organs the hysterectomy had removed were only the size of a small fist and two walnuts. But the surgery had taken away something very precious—her ability to have babies.

And maybe her womanhood along with it.

And every morning she wondered if she was ever going to stop feeling that way.

"Well, standing here staring at it won't make it disappear," she told herself.

Straightening her shoulders, she opened the door and went across the hall to her bedroom, doing what she always did to escape the feelings—turning her thoughts to the day ahead as she pulled on her striped bathrobe.

It was two hours yet before she had to open the store. She'd gotten up early to put the soup ingredients into the slow cooker and so she headed for the kitchen to do just that.

It was the brightest room in her small house, thanks to a big corner window that caught the sun and spilled it in from two directions.

The whole house was decorated in the country style Kansas preferred and the kitchen was no different. Delft tile lined the wall between the countertops and the upper cupboards; she'd hung matching wallpaper on one of the remaining walls, and an antique baker's cupboard added storage space on the third.

In the center of the room was a matching round pedestal table with four high-backed cane chairs set around it, their seats covered with navy blue calico cushions.

Taking the soup ingredients out of the refrigerator, she set them on the countertop beside the sink and began to clean vegetables. As she did she wondered how Danny... and Linc... were today. And knowing she was going to get to see them tonight chased away any lingering sadness.

In fact, the fleeting image of Linc Heller's face dashed through her mind and set off excited flutters in her stomach.

"Just clean the chicken," she ordered herself wryly.

But still she couldn't help wishing for the day to pass quickly.

When the soup was going and the mess cleaned, she fixed herself toast for breakfast and sat down at the kitchen table to eat it. While she did, she flipped through the family album she'd dug out the night before.

The opening pages were photographs of her parents' wedding. Then, just as in real life, soon after that began pictures of Della, then Della and Virgie, and finally Kansas, too. Most of them were unposed shots of birthdays, holidays, family gatherings, vacations. All like a trail up through the years.

It was Virgie who Kansas noticed most in the photos, mainly because she was always making a funny— or not so funny—face, instead of just smiling like everyone else. Or she'd stuck her tongue out, or held her fingers in a horn sign behind someone's head, or just generally been cutting up.

That was Virgie.

The older Virgie got in the pictures, the saucier the poses, as she slipped a T-shirt off her shoulder, jutted a hip out in a vamp stance, or did a Marilyn Monroe pout. Kansas remembered the occasion of some of those photographs and that Virgie had always waited until the last minute, just before the picture was taken, to do those things. Otherwise their parents would never have allowed them.

"Mama always said you were giving her gray hair," Kansas muttered as if her sister could hear her.

Virgie's growing-up years had been hard on the whole family. She'd done every rebellious, outrageous, antagonistic thing she could think of and turned their home into a war zone between herself and their parents most of the time. And now, as Kansas looked at the old pictures, she better understood one of her folks' concerns. Her sister's clothes, makeup and attitude had been much, much too suggestive.

"But the boys all like it," Kansas said out loud, mimicking the angry retort she remembered as her sister's side of the argument.

The boys had definitely liked it. They'd come around in droves.

Until Linc Heller had noticed Virgie.

And Virgie had noticed Linc Heller.

From that moment on, Virgie had shunned every other boy and concentrated solely on Linc.

Kansas flipped a page in the album and there he was. Lincoln Heller. At Della's high school graduation party, his arm around Virgie's shoulders.

Virgie was staring daggers at the camera, but Linc was smiling that thousand-watt smile of his.

Just looking at the photograph gave Kansas a tiny shiver, the same sort of shiver she'd felt as a girl when Linc had turned that charm her way.

But her parents hadn't approved of him. Hell-raiser Heller, everyone had called him, and it had seemed to the elder Dayes that Elk Creek's wildest teenage boy was not an improvement over having whole groups courting their middle daughter.

Kansas had certainly liked Linc better. Everyone else had treated her as the nuisance she was, being so much younger and entertaining herself with spying or openly hanging around. But not Linc. He'd teased her kindly, and flattered her enough to secretly thrill the girl hiding beneath the tomboy.

"And you weren't immune, either, Della, you big fake," she said to a picture that showed her oldest sister watching him with moony eyes. "I should let you see this to prove I was right—you had a crush on him the same as every other girl in town."

But Della wouldn't appreciate that and so Kansas just turned to the last page of the album. Pictures of Della's wedding were encased there. And again, there were shots of Virgie and Linc. The last pictures. The last time anyone in their family had seen Virgie alive.

Kansas touched her fingertips to her sister's image—the only one in which Virgie was simply smiling. Maybe because she'd known she was about to leave behind Elk Creek and the family that she'd considered too dull.

Linc's handsome face still stared from the photograph and suddenly into Kansas's mind came a vivid memory of his kiss from the night before and with it a fresh onslaught of the confusion it had erupted in her.

The man had been her *sister's husband.*

But what if he hadn't been? What if Linc Heller had left Elk Creek alone so many years ago, done his rodeoing and come back now, on his own? All six feet, broad-shouldered, swaggering, rugged-faced, dented-chin, blue-eyed hunk of him. To bathe her in his charm. Would that change anything?

It wouldn't change how attracted Kansas was to him, because she couldn't be any more attracted to him, she admitted secretly.

But it also wouldn't change the fact that Lincoln Heller and Kansas Daye were very different people, who lived very different lives.

It wouldn't change that he was still Hell-raiser Heller and she was quiet Kansas. Or that the two couldn't possibly go together. Any more than pickles and peanut butter.

Or french fries and fruitcake.

Or corn dogs and cream cheese.

He was wild and free spirited and impulsive.

She was calm and conventional and completely predictable.

"Well, maybe not completely predictable," Kansas said to herself.

Because no one could have predicted that quiet, calm, conventional Kansas would have been up most of the night before with fantasies hot enough to melt metal, or that when Linc had kissed her forehead she'd had the urge to reach up and kiss his lips...

Not even Kansas herself could have predicted that.

But still, the fact that her attraction to Linc brought out a little naughtiness in her didn't change that he was not the man for her. Or that she wasn't woman enough for him.

She closed the album with a resounding slam and pushed it away, reminding herself that he *hadn't* kissed her on the lips and that if she had kissed him, she'd have probably made a fool of herself.

A man like Linc wouldn't be interested in a woman like her. He wouldn't even realize she was thinking about him in this way. Certainly he wouldn't be thinking about her as anything but his late wife's little sister, someone whose forehead he could kiss without it meaning a single thing.

Considering it like that made her attraction to him seem more along the lines of that old schoolgirl crush after all. And that was something she could ignore until it passed, couldn't she?

Of course she could.

Though it would help if she didn't have to see him.

But not seeing him meant not seeing Danny and that she couldn't do.

Her nieces and nephews were the closest Kansas might ever come to having kids of her own, and they were important to her. She couldn't stay away from them no matter what. She'd just have to concentrate on getting to know Danny and keep Linc as separate from that as she could.

And yet, as she put the album back into the bookcase in the living room and checked the time to count how many hours would have to pass before she could head for the Heller ranch again, it wasn't Danny alone whom she was thinking about seeing at the end of the day.

Linc would be there, too. Just as surely as he was in her thoughts at that moment, in spite of it all.

As was the case most mornings, Linc was not quite awake but not quite asleep when Danny came into his room. The small child climbed onto his bed, kneeled beside him so close that two bony knees jabbed him in the ribs and gave a little bounce.

Linc opened his eyes only a slit, spying on his son. Danny settled in to watching him and gave a few more bounces that poked his knees into Linc's side before announcing, "I wan' bres'fast."

Linc gave a great big growl, rose up enough to wrap his arms around the boy and pulled him down on top of him in a bear hug that made Danny giggle.

Linc could tell just from touching him that Danny wasn't feverish anymore. "How do you feel this morning?"

"Bedder."

"Me, too." Actually, Linc felt fine.

"I wan' 'cakes wis jowlly."

"Yep, you're better, all right."

"Yep." Danny wiggled out of his father's arms, slid off the bed and stood waiting expectantly. "I wan' 'cakes wis jowlly *now.*"

"Threatened by a three-year-old," Linc muttered to himself as he rolled to the bedside and swung his feet over the edge.

Seeing this, Danny turned around and left the room.

"Not even a three-year-old yet," Linc went on muttering. "I ride the meanest broncs in the country without a qualm, but one threat from a pint-size dictator and I'm up and at 'em."

And he was, too. He pulled on his jeans from the day before, zipped them halfway and went out to the kitchen.

Danny had dragged a chair to the butcher block, climbed up and sat cross-legged and stoic in the middle of it. "I'm really hun'ry."

Linc chuckled and ruffled his son's already tousled hair. "Pancakes it is," he said as he went to the freezer.

"An' jowlly," Danny reminded.

"And jelly."

Linc slid a stack of frozen pancakes onto a plate, popped them into the microwave oven and started it. Then he laid a flat palm against the top of the appliance, closed his eyes and said, "Bless whoever invented this."

"Bless you," Danny repeated as if Linc had sneezed.

"Thanks," Linc answered with a laugh.

He gathered jelly, milk and what was left of their orange juice and brought them to the butcher block. That was when he pressed a hand to his son's forehead just to be sure. "Nope, no fever."

The microwave stopped and Linc took out Danny's pancakes. While he spread jelly on them and cut them into bite-size pieces, he got to thinking about Kansas bringing soup over tonight. He ought to give her a call before she made it and let her know she didn't have to do it now that they weren't sick anymore.

Of course, that would mean she wouldn't be coming over.

"Good 'cakes," Danny informed him. The boy was ignoring the fork and picking up each piece with his fingers, making himself a sticky mess. "Wan' some?" he offered, holding out a section to his father.

Linc let him feed him, then said, "Soup sound good to you for supper tonight?"

"No. I wan' ice cream."

Linc just rolled his eyes at that, pushed away from the butcher block and headed for the phone.

But before he reached it, he detoured to the coffeemaker.

She's not your type, he told himself as he filled the pot. And he knew it was true.

But he recognized this feeling he had deep down inside—he was starting up with Kansas whether she was his type or not.

What he didn't understand was why.

She was beautiful, all right. There wasn't a doubt about that. All fresh-faced and clean and bright as a spring day.

But she was also his late wife's kid sister. And the kind of woman a man didn't mess with unless he had serious intentions, unless he was looking for a serious relationship.

And Linc wasn't, damn those big green eyes of hers.

A challenge—that's what she was, on top of everything else. A challenge to get past that controlled surface and find out if there was a hot spring beneath it. Because he was betting there was. He was betting that if he'd have kissed her full on the mouth last night he'd have tasted a little of it. And damn it to hell, he'd wanted to. Sick and all. He'd wanted to real bad. Worse than he'd wanted to kiss anyone in a long, long time.

He should definitely stay away from that woman.

Which would mean keeping Danny away, too. And that would defeat one of his main purposes in coming back to Elk Creek.

He wanted the boy to know his family, to get close enough to them so he'd have that family to fill the gap when Linc had to go off rodeoing.

What he should do, he knew, was to let Kansas see all she wanted of Danny, but steer clear of her himself. And he should start that right now, by telling her not to come over tonight.

The coffee was ready and he poured himself a mug of it. Then he turned toward the phone again. But rather than head for it, he leaned his hips back against the counter, crossed one ankle over the other, slid his free hand into the unfastened waistband of his jeans and took a drink of the muddy brew that steamed from the cup.

Go over there and call her. Tell her there's no need for her to bring soup. Tell her she's free to see Danny whenever she wants, that she can pick him up any-time, take him over to her place and bring him home afterward, but make it clear the only thing between us is Danny.

Do it, damn it!

But that feeling was itching at him deep down in-side again.

And there, in his mind's eye, was the image of Kansas. He remembered the smell of her skin and the feel of her brow beneath his lips—

"More 'cakes," Danny demanded.

"Just a second," Linc said, staring at the tele-phone as if the intensity of that glance would relay his message to Kansas to stay away.

"I wan' more 'cakes *now.*"

"Hold your horses."

Linc pushed off the counter's edge and went to the phone. He picked up the receiver and let it hang over his thumb as he poked the first three numbers for in-formation with his index finger.

But that fourth number was slow in coming. In fact, he didn't hit it at all.

Instead, for a moment, he just stood there pointing at it.

Then he slammed the receiver back onto the hook.

And went to the freezer instead.

* * *

Kansas closed the store fifteen minutes late. Then she took her time choosing a gift for Danny and called Loreen at the beauty shop to let her know the permanent rods she'd ordered had come in. And all to convince herself she could control her eagerness to get out to the Heller place.

But controlled or not, she was so eager she could have burst, and by the time she allowed herself to go into the bathroom and change into fresh khaki slacks and a red camp shirt, reapply her blush and lipstick, and run a comb through the ponytail she wore low on her neck, her heart was pounding with anticipation.

The anticipation of seeing Danny, she told herself. Not of seeing Linc, whom she had every intention of barely noticing.

She drove too fast out to the ranch, slowing down only when the house came into sight and she could tell Danny was playing in the courtyard.

He was wearing beat-up cowboy boots so big they had to be an old pair of Linc's, and a Stetson hat that must have had the same origin, because it was ragged, sweat stained and covered from the little boy's eyebrows all the way down to the middle of his back.

There was a stick horse between his knees, but he wasn't merely pretending to gallop on it—he held the reins in one hand, his other was raised in the air and he was jumping and jerking around in a comical frenzy that made Kansas laugh as she gathered a shopping bag and the crock of soup from the rear of her car.

"Don't hurt yourself," she cautioned when she reached the courtyard, stopping to watch the scene she wished she could take movies of.

Danny stopped abruptly and frowned up at her as if she were out of her mind. "I'm ridin' my bun'kin' bronc."

"Like your dad. I thought that's what you were doing."

The little boy nodded solemnly.

"Then you must be feeling better."

"Did you bringed ice cream?" he asked as if being well hinged on the answer.

"Chocolate, just like you wanted."

He dropped the stick horse instantly and headed for the house in a hurry, boots clomping on the tile. "Le's go have some!"

Kansas followed him into the house as far as the entrance, pausing when she heard Linc's deep voice asking what all the ruckus was as he came down the stairs. By then Danny had disappeared into the kitchen.

Linc had on jeans that were less faded than those he'd worn the previous day and a chambray shirt with the sleeves rolled to his elbows. His dark mahogany hair glistened and was without a hat dent. He was clean shaven and as he approached, Kansas caught a whiff of a woodsy after-shave that suited him.

"You don't look sick anymore, either," she observed. But he did look ruggedly handsome enough to make her heart skip a beat.

He grinned at her, his smile lopsided and just a shade devilish. "Must have been all that orange juice. Or maybe that little bit of TLC you brought along. I've never been one to underestimate the powers of a beautiful woman fussing over me. And Danny is his father's son."

"Don't lay it on too thick—I don't want to have to shovel out the living room," Kansas bantered back, flattered in spite of herself.

He leaned over the crock and sniffed. "I thought about calling you to say you didn't have to cook for us, but what kind of a daddy would I be if I denied Danny a meal of homemade soup?"

"I'm glad you didn't. I've been looking forward to seeing him all day."

"Just him?"

Oh, that ornery smile and the sparkle in those blue eyes! Kansas's knees went watery. "Behave yourself, Lincoln Heller," she said as if there were starch in them instead.

"Was I misbehavin'?"

It was a sure sign he was only pretending innocence when he dropped the *g's* from his words, but he was still as close to irresistible as any man Kansas had ever known. And as incorrigible, too. "Don't forget," she warned, "I've known you a long time."

He took the crock from her and, while he was at it, bent in close to her ear. "Don't be too sure. And don't ever tell me to behave unless you want just the opposite," he warned back, and his had more power for all its softness, because it sent a shiver up her spine. Or maybe it was the feel of his warm breath against her skin...

Kansas tried not to notice.

In a blaze of newfound courage, though, she said, "Since you're well and I did the cooking, you can get things ready while I play with your son."

"Fair enough. What needs to be done?"

"Heat the soup a little more, and..." She opened the bag and took from it a gaily wrapped package before handing the sack to him, too. "Put the ice cream in the freezer, warm and slice the bread, and pour some dressing over the salad."

Linc pointed his cleft chin at the present. "What's that?"

"A bribe to win Danny's heart," she said with her nose slightly in the air.

He pecked a kiss there before she knew he was going to. "I don't think you need to bribe any man for that, darlin'."

And then he turned and headed for the kitchen while Kansas was still in the throes of a sparkle raining all through her to match the one in his eyes.

She fought the sensation and followed him. When she got there, she found Danny had climbed from a chair to stand on the countertop.

"I'm gittin' mine ice-cream bowl," he informed them both.

"First you're going to eat dinner, my boy," Linc answered him. "And while I get that all set, you can open what your Aunt Kansas brought you."

"A present?" Danny exclaimed as he caught sight of the package Kansas held. He set the bowl down with a clatter and climbed from the counter to the chair to the floor in a big hurry.

"Take your aunt onto the patio. You can open it there and show her Charlie." Then to Kansas he said, "We can eat back there, too. I'll bring everything out when it's ready."

Patio was an understatement for what was behind the Heller house, as Kansas recalled. And she remembered right. From the back door off the kitchen to the east was a bunkhouse that hadn't been used in years, and beside that, a barn and chicken coop. But to the west side was a full eight hundred square feet of brick paving where there were enough tables, lawn chairs and loungers provided for a large garden party should one break out at any moment.

There was also a net hammock to one side and an enormous bricked-in barbecue with a pit next to it big enough to roast a full side of beef. Beyond that was a swimming pool bigger than the public one attached to the town recreation center.

The patio and the side of the house were shaded by age-old black oak trees, their branches already so full of dark maroon leaves that sunlight didn't make more than a fleeting appearance until the limbs dwindled near the pool.

Danny had left his boots and hat on the kitchen floor beside the chair he'd used to climb and now padded ahead of Kansas in his stocking feet. He had on a pair of the smallest jeans she'd ever seen and a striped T-shirt, and he went no more than a yard onto the patio before turning to her.

"Can I open it now?"

Kansas handed the gift to him. In a matter of a few seconds of paper tearing, he'd found the ultimate bubble-making kit inside.

His little face scrunched up in confusion. "What is it?"

Bubbles were one of Kansas's favorite things to give her nieces and nephews because then she got to play with them. She was only too happy to sit cross-legged on the bricks and demonstrate.

Big bubbles. Small bubbles. Cascades of bubbles. Heart shaped. Tubular. Frothy. Bubbles gurgled up from the bowl of a pipe. Bubbles shot from a gun.

Bubbles squeezed out a fat man's mouth. Bubbles everywhere.

Kansas was blowing them from a long strawlike tube and Danny was giggling and chasing them when Linc came out to set one of the tables. He didn't say anything, but she could feel him watching them. When she glanced up at him, his eyes met hers and he smiled a small, closed-lipped smile that said he didn't expect to see her like that.

Kansas raised her chin and blew an insolent plume of iridescent bubbles his way, turning his smile to a grin. A single particularly resilient orb made it all the way to him, and without taking his gaze off her, he caught it with an easy swipe of one big hand and then brought that closed fist to his chest as if he'd snatched something she'd sent him and held it to his heart.

Incorrigible. He was definitely incorrigible.

Then, as if he could read her thoughts, his smile turned knowing. "I'm bringing the food out next, so come and eat, kids."

While he disappeared inside once more, Kansas wrangled with the reluctant Danny, promising him more bubble play after he'd eaten and reminding him there was ice cream for dessert.

She had the little boy sitting at the table by the time Linc came back with a tray full of food.

"I wan' Kansas to sit by me," he informed his father then, as if Linc might take her away.

Linc glanced at her while he unloaded the tray. "Looks like your bribe worked."

"Every time," she answered as if she'd never had a doubt, surprised at her own bolder banter and at how comfortable she was becoming around him.

Danny wanted his soup and salad served by her, and she obliged, using her new leverage to persuade him to eat. Then she sat beside him with her own food, directly across the table from Linc and those cornflower-blue eyes of his that seemed to spend more time watching her than what he was doing.

"Danny was out front riding his 'bunkin' bronc' when I got here," she said to make conversation and avert some of his study of her.

"I maded a whole eight, Dad," he added matter-of-factly.

"A whole eight?" Kansas repeated.

Linc frowned at her in mock disbelief. "Don't you know anything about rodeoing?"

"A little. I've been to Frontier Days. But you forget, I'm a townie, not a cowgirl. I know people ride wild horses and bulls, and race around barrels, and compete with roping and tying and things like that, but I'm not up on the details."

"Danny's talking about the eight seconds a rider has to stay on the back of whatever's tryin' to kick him off."

"Only eight seconds?"

Linc put his face in his hand and laughed. "*Only* eight seconds." Then he looked her in the eye again. "They're the longest, hardest eight seconds of my life."

"I'm sure. I just thought you had to stay on longer than that—like a minute or two."

"Sometimes it's impossible to last even the eight seconds," he said wryly.

"You can," Danny added proudly.

Linc inclined his head in his son's direction but his gaze stayed on Kansas. "The president of my fan club," he joked.

"I've heard you're pretty good, though. The *Gazette* wrote a small article a while ago about some competition in Las Vegas, wasn't it? Said you not only won but got some sort of endorsement out of it, like basketball players get for sneakers."

"Vegas holds the National Finals Rodeo every year—the NFR. That's the grand finale and the biggest prize money."

"And you won that?"

"Yep," Danny answered for him.

"I won the saddle bronc riding event," Linc qualified.

"And the endorsement? What's that for?"

"Boots, hats, Western gear. I'll be posing for some ads, wear their stuff when I ride, things like that."

It was a good choice on the part of the company, Kansas thought, whether or not he'd won any rodeos. He was tall, lean but muscular, and ruggedly gorgeous enough to make anything he wore look good. Or nothing at all? she wondered.

Suddenly her mind pictured an underwear ad a baseball player had done, only instead of the baseball player, she had an image of Linc . . .

Lord, what was she doing? She was undressing the man!

"He gots new boots," Danny volunteered with awe, giving her an escape from her own thoughts.

"Is riding the bucking horse for eight seconds your only event?" Kansas asked to keep herself on the straight and narrow.

"I used to do a little of a lot of things—roping, bull riding, steer wrestling. But now I stick mainly with the broncs and an occasional bull, training just for them."

"Training?"

"It is a genuine sport, Kansas. And keeping fit cuts down on the injuries. I know the reputation of a rodeo cowboy—smoking, drinking, raising hell, carousing all night long, rodeoing just to show off. Maybe that's how it was a while back, but it's serious competition now. We all work out to keep in shape."

He was definitely in shape. Glorious shape. His shoulders were wide and hard, his waist narrow, and even his forearms were tight and sinewy and somehow very sexy sliding out from those rolled-up sleeves. And his hands—they were something all on their own. Great big, strong, masculine hands that were gentle enough to tend his son, gentle enough to have guided her own face back to him at the door the night before...

Kansas forced her gaze from his hands and her thoughts from what they would feel like on other parts of her body, meeting his eyes again. "Doesn't it hurt to be bounced and jarred on the back of a wild animal? Especially—" She cut herself short, realizing at the last minute what she was thinking now and that she didn't have any business wondering about his private parts hitting the saddle.

But clearly he knew what she'd been about to say, because his grin was full of the devil again. "A person can get pretty banged up, break bones, take some serious falls. But we do wear what *protection* we can so we don't all end up childless," he said, nodding once again at Danny as proof.

Kansas could feel her face flaming and she had no one to blame but herself. She steadfastly ate soup, staring into her bowl as she did, trying to will the color out of her cheeks, and hoping the setting sun was low enough to offer some camouflage.

Suddenly drops of cold water splashed against her heated skin, and she glanced up reflexively to find his handsome face alight with amusement, his long, thick fingers poised to splash her a second time.

"It's all right, darlin'," he cajoled just before he laughed outright and lured a smile out of her after all. Then he altered the subject for her. "I myself have broken a dozen different bones and had one concussion that some people were hoping would knock some sense into me. Unfortunately it didn't."

"He got a blacked eye for Christmas," Danny interjected.

"And you really *like* it—roaming around the country, living out of a suitcase, taking physical abuse to make a living?" Kansas asked, feeling her blush recede by degrees.

This time he smiled, it beamed from his face as pure joy. "Love it. Well, I don't love the traveling or the hotels anymore, but gettin' on the back of that bronc while it's still in the chute, I can feel the power and energy between my legs, and I know that animal is going to take me on the ride of my life trying to beat me. But if I can just hang on, I can beat it. And when I do—whoo-ee! Nothin' like it in the world. There's so much adrenaline rushing through my veins I wouldn't feel it if a truck hit me right then." He laughed at himself. "Course, half an hour later and the next day is another story."

"But it's worth it to you?"

"Every bump and bruise and broken bone. And even a few of those unmentionables when they happen."

Oh, he'd enjoyed throwing in that last part! Kansas dunked her fingers into her water glass and splashed him.

Whether or not Danny had seen Linc do it to Kansas, he definitely saw her counterattack and promptly stuck his whole hand in his milk and dumped it over.

"Now look what you caused," Linc accused, but only mockingly. "I'll get a towel."

Kansas was chasing milk with napkins all the way across the table when he came back. Her first sight was of his zipper as he reached the table's edge. And she looked, too. Though not without wondering what had gotten into her tonight.

Linc pitched in with the towel, but it took Kansas a while to realize he was toying with her even in that, playing cat and mouse with her efforts to clean up by following her hands with his so wherever she mopped she bumped into him.

When it finally dawned on her, she retreated altogether.

"Why don't I dish out the ice cream while you finish up here?"

"No fun," he complained with orneriness in his voice, looking at her from beneath his brows.

But Kansas escaped to the kitchen anyway.

Taking the ice cream from the freezer brought a gust of cold air to her face, letting her know just how heated her skin was again, and she reminded herself she was not here to play flirting games with Linc Heller. She was here to be with Danny.

But as she scooped the ice cream into the bowls, she couldn't help glancing out the wall of windows on the west side of the kitchen that allowed a full panorama of the patio and pool.

Linc was bent partway over the table, putting the dinner dishes on the tray. His back was to Kansas and her gaze went all on its own to the pockets of the jeans that fit him as if they were made for him, cupping a to-die-for derriere and long legs as thick and powerful as any horse he could have ever ridden.

Into her mind came his words about having one of those beasts between his thighs, and all at once she wondered just what it would be like to be in that position....

Then he glanced over his shoulder and caught her staring, and she quickly went back to the ice cream, glad when she could return the carton to the freezer and let the cold air from there cool her off yet again.

She ought to go home, she told herself. She ought to leave Linc and Danny to their dessert and escape before this heightened awareness of Linc got any worse tonight.

But no matter what she knew she ought to do, she picked up the bowls and went back out to the patio.

It was dark by then and Linc had switched on the tall wrought-iron Victorian-style street lamps that surrounded the area, bathing it in creamy light.

"Did you show your Aunt Kansas Charlie?" he asked Danny then.

"Nope," the little boy answered, but after a bite of dessert he explained that Charlie was his bunny.

And while Danny ate and turned into a chatterbox about his new pet, Kansas felt Linc watching her. She knew it without even looking his way. She could feel his gaze as if it were something tangible. Feel him studying her hair, caressing her face, dropping to her breasts...

Or was she just imagining that he was thinking the same kinds of things about her that she'd been thinking about him all evening?

When they'd finished eating, Linc announced it was Danny's bedtime. Danny pitched a fit and was appeased only when Linc conceded to him introducing Kansas to Charlie after all, and then letting Kansas put him to bed.

"I'll clean up the dinner mess, if you'll do that," Linc told her.

Kansas didn't need persuading; she was thrilled.

"Danny can put on his own pajamas and brush his teeth," Linc explained when she'd assured him she didn't mind the chore. "Then he turns on a star machine he has and you need to tell him a story—'The Three Little Pigs' or 'Goldilocks,' something like that. He'll fall right to sleep."

With the instructions given, Danny took her hand and tugged her to the rabbit hutch out near the chicken coop.

Charlie was an adorable brown lop-eared bunny that Danny informed her couldn't be held without Linc there.

"We could only pet his nose," the little boy told her solemnly, and they both did just that.

Then Danny led the way back into the house and upstairs to his room.

While he did what he was supposed to in the connecting bathroom, Kansas rolled back the bedcovers and fluffed his pillow.

He came out much sooner than a good teeth-brushing would have required, but she let him get away with it. Instead she just watched as he gathered the raggedy blanket he'd had with him the night before and flicked a switch on a small box on the dresser. He couldn't reach the light switch, so Kansas turned that off, leaving the room in darkness except for a rotating array of star-dots projected onto the ceiling.

"What a nice way to fall asleep," she said, enjoying the display.

"It's like campin', my dad says, and I can see the same thing ev'ry night no matter where we're sleepin'."

Every time Danny referred to his dad, Kansas realized, it was with an adoration that confirmed just what a good father Linc was. She couldn't help wondering if Virgie had been or would have been as good at parenting as Linc had settled into being, despite his wandering ways, remembering that her sister had never been particularly fond of kids and had even refused to baby-sit as a teenager.

Danny climbed into bed, wiggled around until he found just the right spot, adjusted his covers and then the security blanket so that he had an index finger inside one corner of the satin edging and his thumb ready for sucking.

Once everything was just so, he told Kansas she had to lie down beside him so she could see the stars, too, while she told him a story.

Kansas was more than happy to oblige, laying her head beside her nephew's on the pillow, feeling the warmth of his tiny body at her side. She longed to hold him, smooth his hair from his brow, but thought it was too soon yet and contented herself with this much.

"Do you know the shinny-shin-shin one?" Danny
asked then.

"The story of 'The Three Little Pigs?' I think so."

"Tha's the one I wan' tonight." He stuck his thumb
into his mouth, began to rub the tip of his nose with
his satin-encased finger and stared up at the stars.

Kansas's heart swelled just looking at him. She
started the story only to have him stop her and point
at the ceiling.

"Look there," he said with a mouthful of thumb.

"Oh. I'm sorry," she apologized with the same solemnity he'd used to instruct her, turning her head and
going on.

By the time the short tale was over, Danny had
fallen asleep and his head had curved down to Kansas's shoulder. It was a blissful feeling to her and she
couldn't give it up just yet, so she stayed where she
was.

The bed was very soft. Danny's breath feathered
against her neck and she watched the stars rotate in the
ceiling sky, round and round, in a hypnotizing crawl,
thinking what a good idea of Linc's the machine
was...

"Kansas?"

A deep, sensuous voice called her name in a bare
whisper, near enough to her ear that she could feel the
warmth of the word. And there were soft strokes of
her temple that trailed into her hair, again and again,
and made it hard to want to wake up.

"You're welcome to spend the night, darlin', but if
you're going to, you'd better let me take off your shoes
at least," the voice said with an underlying layer of
amusement to it now.

Linc. It was Linc's voice.

Kansas opened her eyes with a jolt and turned her head to find his face mere inches from her own.

How did he get in her bedroom? was her first panicked thought.

Then she realized she wasn't in her own bedroom and remembered Danny and the star machine.

"Oh!" she whispered, bolting to a sitting position while her eyes tried to focus, and her brain swam up from the depths of sleep.

"It's all right," Linc assured in a voice that seemed as quiet and intimate as the night. "I should have warned you about lying down with him and looking up at the stars. It'll put you to sleep every time."

Still, Kansas felt foolish. And sleep fuzzy. Too fuzzy to resist when Linc took her hand and led her out of the room and down the stairs.

She couldn't have been asleep long, could she have?

Long enough, she realized, for him to have turned on the stereo so low it was barely audible and pulled all the drapes in the living room.

"I'd better go home," she said, only a few feet from the bottom of the stairs, before he could lead her astray.

Linc stopped short and turned to face her. Kansas took two steps away from him and came up against the newel post.

"Are you afraid of me, little Kansas?" he asked in the same voice he'd used in Danny's room—honey roasted, quiet and amused, too, as he stretched just one arm out to grab the stair railing behind her and lean his weight on it.

"Nooo," she said as if the very idea were ludicrous. But she was afraid. Of her own attraction to him. Of what a man like him would want with a woman like her. Of how easy it might be for him to get it . . .

"I think you are," he said with a slight chuckle.

"Should I be?" she challenged.

One eyebrow shrugged upward, but he said, "I don't think so."

Lord, why did he have to be so good-looking? And smell like the woods in winter? And have those cornflower-blue eyes that seemed to slip inside her and laugh at her and caress her all at once? And those lips—full and devilish and promising pleasures she could only imagine . . .

"I have to go!"

He cocked his head to one side in response, but pushed off the banister and gave her room to do just that. "Whatever you say."

She was acting like a lunatic, she decided on the way to the front door. And it was all due to the things that had been going through her mind about him tonight.

But none of it was because of anything he'd done or said and so there was no way he could understand it. Tamping down on what she considered her own silliness, she decided to get a grip before she made a complete fool of herself.

"I'm crazy about Danny," she said as she stepped out into the courtyard, after taking a few deep breaths of cool night air.

"Looks like he's feeling the same way," Linc said. "That's the first time he's ever wanted anyone but me to put him to bed."

"I don't think he brushed his teeth too well, though," she admitted.

Something about that made him smile. "I'll take care of it in the morning." He didn't say anything else, though. He just stood there, watching her, seeming to find something quietly amusing.

"Well, I'd better go."

"I think you'd probably better," he challenged.

"It's just that it isn't a good idea for you and I to..." To what? Lord, she was making this worse. Falling asleep had clouded her brain and it had been foggy with thoughts of him even before that.

But he said, "I know," as if he really did understand what she was talking about. "I keep telling myself the same thing."

He took a step nearer to her anyway, closing the distance between them, and reached both hands to cup the back of her head. He brought her all the way up to her toes, bending his wonderful face to hers and capturing her eyes with his for one long, deep, soul-searching moment before his mouth covered hers in a kiss that was definitely not a meaningless forehead buss for a sister-in-law.

Kansas closed her eyes even while she told herself to push away. His lush lips parted and drew hers along with them as he kissed her so thoroughly she felt as if it were the first time she'd ever been kissed at all.

And then, just as she was marveling at it, he let her go, first with his mouth, then with his hands, and stepped back to where he'd been before.

He pointed that dented chin of his at her car and said, "Go on home, Kansas. Go on," as if he were battling the same thing she was and needed her to leave to keep control over it.

She turned and went to her car, getting in and locking the door before she even glanced in his direction again.

When she did, she found him standing at the edge of the courtyard, feet spread apart, all his weight slung on one hip. His hands were jammed insolently into his pockets, his thumbs pointing at that portion of his body that had repeatedly caught her attention throughout the evening. His moonlight-gilded hair looked as if he'd dragged his hands through it just since she'd turned away from him.

And Kansas wanted to go back for more of the kiss that had been much, much too brief. She wanted it so strongly that she knew it couldn't be good for her.

She started the engine, turned on her lights and put the car into gear. Only then did she glance once more at Linc, shaking her head back and forth so fiercely it was as if she were answering something he'd said.

But what she was really saying no to was herself and her own attraction to him.

Chapter Four

It was hard to sleep through a helicopter landing close by, so Linc knew Jackson had come home in the middle of the night. Apparently Danny knew it, too, because Linc heard the little boy bypass his room the next morning to join his uncle in the kitchen.

Jackson made it a point to come to a few rodeos each year to see Linc and spend some time with him and Danny, so Jackson was the sole member of the boy's family whom he knew before coming back to Elk Creek. And when Linc found his son and his brother after indulging in an extra hour of sleep himself, Jackson was teaching the boy to tie knots, using kitchen twine instead of rope to accommodate Danny's tiny hands.

"Mornin'," Linc greeted them both at once.

"Mornin'," Jackson answered.

"Look'ut I did," Danny said, holding up what looked like an attempt at a bowline knot.

"Good job," Linc proclaimed after duly studying his son's lopsided handiwork.

"There's coffee and biscuits," Jackson informed him.

His brother made lighter, fluffier biscuits than any Linc had ever eaten anywhere. He put five on a plate, slathered them with gravy and poured himself a mug of steaming coffee. Then he brought everything to the trestle table where Jackson sat with the remains of his and Danny's breakfast.

While Danny was on the floor concentrating mightily on yet another knot, Jackson turned to Linc.

"Sorry about landing so late last night, but I was anxious to get home. Four days away is more than I care for."

Linc nodded as he chewed a mouthful of food. There were a lot of ways he and Jackson differed, and this was the biggest. While Linc was happy wandering from place to place, Jackson seemed to have been born with mile-deep roots in the ranch.

It was like a beloved wife and family to him. He worked for it, lived for it, cherished it. And he'd been running it alone since he was twenty-two and their father had retired—fifteen years ago.

It really was Jackson's ranch, no matter what the will said. That was how Linc saw it and he thought that was how their sister, Beth, saw it, too.

But Jackson didn't seem to mind that the other two Hellers had inherited a portion of it equal to his own. He didn't even sit at the head of the table now, as he well might have. Instead it was Danny's breakfast that littered that spot while Jackson sat around the corner from it.

"Danny's grown since I saw him last," Jackson said, sliding his chair out so he could prop one leg over the corner of the table and the other leg over that one, taking his own coffee mug to brace against his flat stomach.

"You haven't seen him since Vegas—that's nearly half a year," Linc reminded.

Linc knew that he and Jackson resembled each other. He didn't notice it himself but enough people had commented on it to bring it to his attention, though Linc thought his brother was probably the better-looking of the two of them. They were the same size, the same build, but while Linc's muscles came out of a gym and off the back of bucking broncos, Jackson's came from just plain hard work that he did alongside the ranch hands he employed.

"I was coming to the rodeo in Nebraska but then I got the news about Shag and there were things to see to," Jackson explained.

Nebraska was where he'd tracked Linc down to tell him the news that their father had died.

Samuel Thomas Heller. Shag.

One of the strictest, sternest, orneriest, most cantankerous old cusses to ever live. There hadn't been a soft spot in the man, at least not one any of his three children had ever seen. Their mother had died when they were all still young and Shag had raised them alone, never sparing the rod, not even on Beth, his only daughter. He'd worked them all worse than any hired hand, tolerated no weakness or whining, and expected them to toe the line.

So, of course, they'd all rebelled and brought down even more on their heads by way of punishment.

The day Beth—the youngest—went off to college, he'd turned the place over to Jackson, as if he'd hung on to it simply for their sake, and spent most of his time from then on traveling, stopping back in Elk Creek only periodically during any year.

All Linc or Jackson or Beth had known about what he did or where he went was that if they ever needed to reach him they were to leave a message with an attorney in Denver because he was there more than he was anywhere, visiting a lady friend.

And "lady friend" was the sum and substance of what any of them knew about whoever it was that drew Shag to Colorado.

He might have been a contrary, stubborn bear of a man, but he'd had a strong moral code he'd lived by. He'd gone to his grave contending that his children should never see him with a woman other than their mother.

"Did you know Shag wanted to be cremated and interred before we were even told he'd died?" Linc asked.

Jackson shook his head in a solemn back-and-forth motion. "No idea."

"I thought his funeral might give us a chance to finally meet the woman he kept company with."

Jackson frowned ominously. "I'm figuring she's the Ally Brooks in the will, how about you?"

"Seems likely. Why else would he have left her a full quarter share of everything he owned?"

"The lawyer says he sent word to her but hasn't heard back. Seems strange to me. She was in bed with him when he died, saw to his last wishes and yet hasn't come around to find out what she inherited."

"Could be she knows already and is in no hurry to stake her claim," Linc suggested.

"I left word with the lawyer to make her an offer for her share of the ranch. If you and Beth want in on that, we can split it three ways. But even if you don't, I'm buying her out myself."

Linc nodded his understanding. "I don't want any more of this place than he left me. In fact, I'll sell you my portion if you want."

Again Jackson shook his head. "Wouldn't be right. You and Beth have a stake in the ranch the same as I do, and if you stick around Elk Creek there'll be times I'll work you to remind you of it. It'll always be your home, too, to use or not as you need. But I can't see where some damn woman from Denver has a right to a quarter of it. She can keep her share of everything else. But not the ranch."

"How long do you suppose they were involved before he died?" Linc wondered out loud.

"I think even before he retired, because he hightailed it down there first thing when he did."

"Does Beth know any more about her than we do, do you think?"

"Nope. I asked when I called with the news." Jackson took a drink of his coffee and for a time they let silence settle between them. Then he said, "Beth's coming, you know. We can go over the whole will and what we've inherited when she gets here."

"Is she bringing her husband?"

"Don't know. There's something strange going on. Took me three days of leaving messages before I finally got Ash on the phone and he wasn't any too friendly—acted like he didn't want to talk to me. I thought maybe he'd break the news about old Shag to Beth, but he just said I'd have to reach her at another number and rattled it off."

"At another number?" Linc repeated. "You mean like a work number, or is she living somewhere else?"

"Not a work number. She was at someone named Celia's."

"Living there?"

"Beth wouldn't tell me a thing. But she sounded down in the dumps even before I gave her the news about Shag. Said she hadn't been feeling well, but she wouldn't say what was wrong when I asked. Guess we'll find out when she gets here."

Linc finished his biscuits and gravy, sat back and propped his legs on the table much the same way Jackson's were.

Danny went to his uncle just then for help with a new knot, and Linc looked on as his brother patiently showed the little boy what he'd done wrong.

Then Jackson poured both himself and Linc more coffee and returned to his previous position. "Danny says he's seen his Aunt Kansas."

Linc nodded. "He and I were sick when we got in and I had to go to the store for some things." He went on to explain how he'd hooked up with her.

"You've seen Della, too, then? How'd that go?"

Linc shrugged. "She's holding a grudge."

"But Kansas isn't?"

Every time Jackson said her name something thrummed inside Linc. "She doesn't seem to be." And that was all it took to bring her image into his mind as vividly as if she were in the room with him. "She grew up real well," he said in response to what was in his mind's eye.

Jackson's mug stopped halfway to his mouth. He turned to stare at Linc. "I suppose she did," he said, the simple sentence laden with questions.

"And she's already crazy about Danny."

"I understand she's close to Della's kids, too. Like a second mother to them, is what I hear."

"How come she didn't marry and have her own?"

Jackson didn't answer him. Instead he stared at Linc, his eyes narrowed as if he could see through him that way. "Of all the women in this town—of all the women in the *world*—she's about the unlikeliest one for you," he finally said.

"I was only asking about her," Linc contended as if his curiosity weren't part and parcel of just the kind of feelings for her that his brother suspected.

"She's not like Virgie," Jackson warned.

"Never thought she was."

"She's a churchgoer. Helps out at the school. Runs the store. Reads to the old Carter widow once a week. Early to bed, early to rise. Concentrates on doing the right thing—organized a bunch of us to paint houses last summer for those who couldn't afford it or weren't able to do it themselves. She helps with Christmas baskets for the needy, things like that. No all-night dancin' or traipsin' off somewhere on a whim or—"

"I get the picture, Jackson," Linc cut off his brother with exasperation.

But Jackson added anyway, "She's not your type."

"I just asked why she wasn't married with kids of her own. I'm not lookin' to corrupt her, if that's what you're worried about. Are you a little sweet on her yourself?"

Jackson frowned so blackly it put Linc in mind of their father. "She was friends with Beth after you left, hung around here enough for me to get to thinking about her like a little sister. Elk Creek is a small town—there's no way not to hear what everybody's up to. Knowing what kind of woman she is, what she does, doesn't make me sweet on her, no. I'm just saying she isn't your type. Like most folks around here, she leads a quiet life and that's it."

"Like I said, I never thought any different," Linc answered, getting up from the table to clear the breakfast mess.

In fact, part of Kansas's appeal was that very wholesomeness his brother described. But he didn't say that. He didn't say that after all these years of his own wild life, her wholesomeness was very appealing. And discovering that it was peppered with just a dash of spunk, that she could be a little saucy when he coaxed her just right, only made her all the more interesting.

But Jackson seemed to think she was some sort of saint. He didn't seem to know what was waiting just below the surface.

Maybe he also hadn't noticed that sassy rear end that turned Linc's knees to mush, or eyes that glimmered with secret passions, or the chin that challenged him to look past the sainthood to find a little of the sinner underneath.

No, Jackson didn't seem to know any of those things about her.

And there was one other thing Linc would bet his brother didn't know about Kansas Daye.

She surely could kiss.

That took a little coaxing, too, but like the rest of it, it was worth it. In fact, it was all the better because it told him she didn't give it too freely or to too many.

No sir, Jackson must not know that.

Or he'd have been as sweet on her as Linc was. In spite of himself.

The gym in Elk Creek's school was decorated like the inside of a barn. Hay bales were piled here and there around the room and the booths were built to look like stalls. A Down-home Bazaar—that's what the fliers posted all over town were calling this event, the purpose of which was to raise money for computers and to compensate for government budget cuts.

The place was brimming with people that night when Kansas arrived with Della, Bucky and the kids. Most of Elk Creek's citizens had turned out. Not only was it a worthy cause, but also a chance to socialize and an entertaining diversion in a small town that offered few of those.

There were wheel of fortune games, ringtoss, a cakewalk, fishing, blackjack, a shooting gallery, competitions for basketball throwing and horseshoes. A car had been donated to raffle off. Stuffed animals, hams, whole wheels of cheese and coupons for services and merchandise could be won. Baked goods, popcorn, hot dogs, drinks, and spicy peanuts could be bought, as could the kisses of the pretty new third-grade teacher. There was also to be an old-fashioned auction of box suppers.

Teachers, the principal, school secretaries, and some of the parents were running everything, all of them in too-large overalls, bandanna shirts and bare feet, with straw hats atop their heads and freckles drawn across their noses. A few of them chewed toothpicks or single sticks of straw for effect, and all in all the mood was lighthearted.

Kansas's brother-in-law, a short, stocky man, took his and Della's four kids off to the cafeteria, where the fun was aimed at children, and Kansas and Della headed for the table where the box suppers were stacking up. It was a slow progression as they stopped every few steps to say hello to someone and exchange amenities.

As they did, Kansas scanned the faces of these people she knew well. She had no reason to think Linc would come. In fact, she hoped he didn't.

Well, a part of her hoped he didn't.

Then there was that other part of her...

She pushed down on it.

The bazaar could be an entertaining public diversion, but she had no desire to be a private one for Linc Heller.

Della stopped to ask the swimming instructor about signing up her kids for lessons. It wasn't a subject Kansas could even pretend an interest in and so her eyes went on wandering from face to face with a will of their own.

What would she do if he did show up?

Just the thought made her heart flutter.

But she ignored that.

If he were to show up, she'd act no differently than she did toward anyone else. Except that she'd try to stay away from him.

Linc was trouble to a woman like her. After all, what in the world would she do with a sweet-talking ladies' man who traveled the country like a gypsy?

He probably broke hearts in every city he visited.

And what would he want with her, anyway? She was an ordinary woman, living an ordinary small-town life, going to school bazaars where he'd be bored to tears.

It was just that when she was with him, she somehow lost sight of that. When she was with him, she wasn't herself. Certainly she hadn't been thinking like herself to have let him kiss her last night.

That was what she'd decided by the time she'd reached her house afterward. She was not an indiscriminate person. She was not a person who went around kissing just any man. Not even one with eyes that sparkled. Certainly not one for whom kissing her was just a dalliance, something to pass the time until he went on his way again, while it stirred much more serious things in her.

Things that surprised her. Shocked her. Things she didn't know she had in her. Things that, once she'd been back in the safety of her cubbyhole of a house, she didn't think she wanted to know she had in her.

Because knowing they were there, knowing how it felt to have her blood race, her senses sizzle, her head grow light with just a kiss, made it hard to go back to that cubbyhole.

But that cubbyhole was where she belonged.

"If somebody can get ol' Bucky Dennehy up here, we can start auctioning the box suppers and feed some hungry folks," the school principal said into a microphone set up nearby.

Hoots of encouragement answered that and Della hollered out that her husband was in the cafeteria.

"No, I'm not. I'm right here," he called back, making his way through the crowd that cheered him on.

Bucky hopped up onto the riser that served as a stage, taking the microphone in experienced hands. "Where's my Della's supper?" he said right off the bat. "Get me that one first."

The principal searched through the stack until he found it and passed it along to Bucky.

"I'm buyin' this one for twenty-five dollars before we even get started and not givin' any of you other guys a chance at it. My Della makes the best fried chicken and potato salad in the whole state and I'm not riskin' having to share her company, either." He set the box behind him on a higher riser, paid the money to the PTA president and then winked outrageously at his wife. "You can thank me for braggin' on you a little later, honey."

Everyone laughed and Della puckered up and kissed the air in his direction, causing even more of a stir before Bucky got down to business.

There wasn't a large single population in Elk Creek, so most of the suppers were purchased by husbands, turning the auction into a competition to see who thought the most of his wife and her cooking and raising a lot of good-natured teasing.

When the box supper of a single woman came up for auction, interest was stirred to see who would bid for the food and the opportunity to share it with its preparer, though there weren't a lot of surprises there, either.

Kansas wasn't at all anxious for her own turn. There were a few likely bidders but none she cared to eat supper with. She hadn't intended to do this at all, but Della had insisted.

Her sister had said it was time for her to get back onto the dating bandwagon and thought a simple supper here among the whole town was an easy start. In fact, she'd been so determined that she'd threatened to make up a second box herself and just put Kansas's name on it.

Kansas had conceded because it was a good cause, but made Della promise not to leave her alone with Sandy Morton from the gas station or Dave Nolan, the manager of the Dairy King, if either of them bought it.

"Next up we have a delectable repast from my very own sister-in-law, Kansas Daye," Bucky announced then.

Bucky looked directly at her and said, "Did you put some of your fudge in here, Kansas?" Then, before she had a chance to answer, he closed his eyes as if in ecstasy, raised his face heavenward and shook his head. "Mmm-mmm. She makes the finest fudge I have ever tasted in my life. It's cost me a few extra pounds over the years, I'll tell you. Now who's going to start the bidding on a chance to taste it?"

The high-pitched voice of Dave Nolan offered two dollars, making the crowd chuckle and Kansas cringe, both because of whom the bid had come from and how low it was.

"I'll give three," Sandy Morton said as if he were being exceptionally generous.

"I'll give thirty."

A cheer went up and Kansas's heart lurched without even looking to see who the higher bidder was. She didn't have to. The smoked-wood voice of Linc Heller was unmistakable.

There was no doubt that neither the mechanic nor the ice-cream jockey were going to go high enough to counter that bid and everyone knew it.

Kansas closed her eyes as an internal tug-of-war was waged inside of her between the thrill of knowing she was about to have supper with Linc and the knowledge that she should starve rather than get within a hundred yards of that charm.

"Forty dollars!"

Kansas's eyes flew open and her head shot to this last bidder.

"Della!" she said in an urgent whisper, mortified to have her *sister* bidding on her box supper.

But Della didn't even look at her. Instead she stared straight ahead, an intense frown on her face, and called out "Forty-five," upping her own offer before there was even a need.

"You can't afford that!" Kansas argued with the most succinct of the many reasons she wanted to stop her sister, trying not to be overheard as she did.

Nervous chuckles rippled through the crowd and then the sound of a single pair of hard-heeled boots making a confident, steadfast path in Kansas and Della's direction quieted even that.

Linc came to stand on Kansas's opposite side. He leaned slightly around her until his eyes met Della's in a stare-down.

Kansas wanted to take both their heads and knock them together for making such a spectacle out of her.

Locked in silent combat with her sister, Linc called out, "I'll give you a hundred dollars for it, Bucky. And a hundred more than what anybody else bids."

Some joker from the back called out, "A hundred and one," and without missing a beat, Linc said, "Two hundred and one."

"This is ridiculous," Kansas muttered, wanting to crawl into a hole.

"Sold! For two hundred and one dollars to Linc Heller," Bucky said in a hurry.

Della finally broke from looking eye-to-eye with Linc and glanced at Kansas. "You don't have to eat with him."

"It's all right," Kansas said, more conscious of trying to soothe her sister and escape the attention of everyone standing around them than of anything else at that moment.

"I promise I won't bite her, Delaware," Linc said. "In fact, you and Bucky can even sit with us to make sure I mind my manners. I'd be happy for your company."

Kansas watched her sister, wondering what she'd say to that, if she'd get mad and make an even bigger scene or concede to his charm the way she had in the store that first day.

But Della didn't do either. Instead she shook her head sadly, her expression turning to one of pure, poignant fear. "You already used up one of us, Linc. Wasn't that enough?"

Linc sobered and he shook his head, too. "You're wrong, Della. I didn't use up Virgie. And I'm not here to use up Kansas, either. Just to have supper with her while you and the whole town watch."

"I will be watching you, too. Real close."

"I welcome it," he assured her, and it seemed almost as if they'd once again reached some sort of temporary truce. Della took a deep breath and walked to the risers where Bucky had just finished auctioning the last box and was telling everyone to find their partners and enjoy their suppers.

"I'm surprised to see you here," Kansas said then, because it sounded better than *I wish you hadn't come.*

He shrugged a broad shoulder inside a plaid Western shirt. "Saw the signs everywhere and figured Danny'd be using the computers in a couple of years so I should do my part." He paused a moment while those blue eyes of his seemed to drink her in. "And because I was pretty sure you'd be here," he added in a quiet voice that brought a quirk to his lips.

Kansas swallowed hard and tried not to feel flattered. "Where is Danny?"

"With Jackson. They decided they'd rather clean out the helicopter than come." Linc took her hand just then and brought it to the crook of his arm, holding it there. "Come on. I have a bill to settle and some supper to eat."

He was holding tight to her so Kansas couldn't have taken her hand away if she wanted to, which solved that dilemma for her as he headed in the direction of the table. But even without the choice to make, there was a sharp set of contradictions alive inside her.

His being there increased her excitement level a hundredfold. But it also embarrassed her that everyone in the place watched them and whispered. The feel of his hard arm beneath her hand, his hand over hers, just being there so close beside him, put all her senses into overdrive. But she didn't want to feel that way. And certainly not in front of the whole town. Or where it hurt and scared Della.

Linc paid the outrageous amount he'd bid on Kansas's box supper, and while he did, she let go of his arm.

"Come on back here," he ordered good-naturedly.

But before she could say anything about how inappropriate it was, his old friends began to welcome him home and he needed one hand for the supper and the other for shaking.

Linc was a popular rascal, and there weren't many townsfolk who didn't see him as a sort of celebrity. And all of them wanted to say hello. As a result, it took him and Kansas a long while to move through the crowd to three hay bales stacked like stairs in a corner.

When they got there and sat down to eat, he leaned close to her ear and confided, "I've been away as many years as I lived here. Most of these faces are familiar but I'm having some trouble putting names to them or placing them."

Kansas—or anyone else—wouldn't have guessed that by the way he'd responded to each person who had stopped to talk. It was that way of his again, she realized. It wrapped around a person and made him feel like a long-lost friend no matter who he was.

Could the same easy charm that masked what was going on behind it be at work on her, too? she wondered.

And yet she also couldn't help thinking that it wasn't everyone whose box supper he'd just paid two hundred and one dollars for, or whom he'd chosen to be with tonight.

Linc leaned even closer, so close his breath was warm against her skin. "Don't run out on me after we eat. I'm counting on you to help," he said in a tone that was certainly more intimate than anything she'd heard him use with anyone else.

That sense of intimacy was between them in more ways than that, though, Kansas realized. It was there in the way he sat, turned slightly toward her, one of his shoulders behind hers and near enough to press against her. It was there in his big thigh running the length of hers, bracing only half the box while the other half was on her leg. It was there in his sharing of the food she'd packed, going so far as to try hand-feeding her grapes, though she wouldn't let him. It was there in his eyes and the attention he paid her, as if they were alone instead of in a crowded room.

And she knew the feelings it raised inside her were all dangerous.

"Who is that big bald guy? The heavyset one in the green shirt?" he asked when they'd finished eating and he started to study the crowd.

"Vince Warzinski," she said, making it clear she couldn't believe he didn't recognize the man who had been one of his good friends.

"No. Can't be. Bean-pole Warzinski? He barely weighed a hundred and twenty pounds and had hair to his shoulders."

"But he married Bonnie Bray—she fattened him up with breads from her mother's bakery and probably pulled half his hair out through the down-and-dirty fights they have about once a month."

"Bonnie Bray? Where is she?"

Kansas pointed her out to him, relaying the fact that the couple's last argument had sent Bonnie chasing Vince down Center Street with a baseball bat.

"Okay, now, who is that gray-haired woman? Bring me up to date," he said then.

Kansas knew with clear certainty that she should refuse, that she should make up an excuse and leave him to fend for himself rather than sitting cozily in this corner with him.

But she didn't do it. Instead she opened her mouth and out came another story about one of the people he'd left behind.

And the moment it did she could feel her own self-conciousness dissolving as she settled in to having a good time with him.

When the bazaar ended, Linc was still at Kansas's side, where he'd been every minute throughout the evening. Because of that, it didn't seem at all out of place for him to want to take her home.

Kansas secretly admitted to herself that she wasn't any too anxious to lose his company. But she'd come with Della and Bucky, and it seemed only right to leave with them.

"What would you say to my seeing Kansas home?" Linc asked Della as he and Kansas trailed them out, Della and Bucky carrying their two youngest kids and Della pretending Linc was invisible.

"I'd say it was up to Kansas," her sister answered darkly.

"I'd say it was, too," Bucky added, making a joke of it. "Go on, Kansas," he urged then, receiving a hit in the arm for it from his wife.

Linc glanced sideways at Kansas. "Well, what do you say?"

They'd reached the parking lot by then, and as she stood between her sister's car and Linc's truck, Kansas felt torn between Linc and Della, between her own desires and good sense.

"Actually, it's so nice out I think I'll walk home," she announced. Somehow it seemed like a compromise. But it left Linc free to say he'd walk along, which was just what he did, pleasing her deep down in a place she didn't want to acknowledge.

"I'll talk to you tomorrow then," Della said, though somehow there was a warning to Linc in her tone, as if she'd be checking up on just what he did to end this evening, and it had better be something she approved of.

Good-nights were murmured all around, and Kansas and Linc headed across the parking lot. From there all the way past the courthouse, neither of them could say much as cars drove by, with people honking and calling, "Good night," and "Good to see you again," and "Let's get together and raise some hell like old times," to Linc.

It wasn't until they turned onto the side street that led to Kansas's cul-de-sac, that they had a chance to say anything to each other.

"Between your sister and my brother I feel like the serpent offering the apple to Eve," Linc finally mused as they strolled slowly up the middle of the road. But he didn't sound daunted, only amused.

"I understand what's on Della's mind, but why would Jackson have anything to say about... anything?" Kansas had almost said *you and me* but amended it at the last minute because that phrase made them sound so much like a couple. And they weren't a couple. Not at all. They were just two people who'd known each other all their lives and shared a connection to a little boy they both loved.

And as if to confirm it, she widened the distance between them.

Linc glanced at her and raised both his eyebrows in question but only responded to her asking why Jackson should have said anything at all about her. "I have the impression my brother thinks you're some kind of saint. And of course everybody knows I'm a sinner."

"Are you?" Kansas challenged.

He smiled a wicked smile. "Nah. Not anymore."

"Mmm," she muttered as if she were reserving judgment. "But you admit you were?"

"Guess that all depends on what the definition is. I don't lie, cheat or steal. Don't gamble or take up with other men's wives. But I have to admit to some drinking and smoking on occasion, and to getting into some two-fisted disagreements—mostly in my younger days."

He reached across the gap she'd made between them, took her hand and pulled her nearer than she'd been before. Then he enclosed her hand in his, holding it to his chest. "And I've been known to enjoy a walk in the moonlight with a beautiful woman," he added.

"Not a lot of sinning in any of that," she decreed, dismayed to find his touch had softened her voice and put a breathy quality in it.

"What about you? Are you a saint?"

"Not that I've noticed," she said wryly, knowing she should pull away from him and yet giving in to the sinner in her that wanted to stay.

"Good," he answered, bringing her hand up to kiss her knuckles. "Then I don't have to worry about corrupting you."

Kansas laughed, not only in response to what he said but to the scattershot of sparks his kiss sent up her arm. "How exactly would you corrupt me?"

Transferring her hand to his other one, he still held it to his broad, hard chest, but put his free arm around her, drawing her into his side. "Seems Della's afraid I'll lure you away from Elk Creek," he suggested.

"I love Elk Creek. I can't be lured away."

"I could take up so much of your time there wouldn't be any left over for reading to widows or painting houses for the needy."

The fractious part of her shouted *Yes, yes, yes, spend that much time with me!* But Kansas tamped down on it and said, "Or you could join in the painting. We always need another pair of hands."

"Ah . . . there's a side our siblings didn't consider— you could reform me."

"Could I?" she bantered boldly, glancing at him from the corner of her eye as they headed for her house.

His smile was slow and sensual. "I think you might just be able to do anything you wanted with me."

"Be careful. Don't assume a saint like me couldn't want anything too sinful. I could surprise you."

He laughed full out at that, as if the rejoinder alone had surprised him. It was a glorious, full-barreled sound that echoed against her neighbors' houses as they went up her walk.

Kansas's house was a white clapboard with a second story smaller than the first and a high-pitched roof. Six wide steps rose up to a front porch with a carved railing and posts and ornate gables lining the overhang.

She took pride in the place, and the porch showed that in the ivy that grew up the poles and along the gables; in the white wicker table, the matching wicker chairs and swing with their flowered seat cushions; even in the beribboned wreath that hung on the crossbar of the old-fashioned screen door.

"Yes, please, surprise me," he pretended to beg as they climbed the steps. Then, in a teasing tone, he said, "In fact, you could start by inviting me in."

"Now, that did sound like a sinner trying to corrupt a saint."

"It could be fun," he tempted, raising just one eyebrow at her this time.

"It could be. But it won't, because it isn't going to happen," she answered, fighting a smile along with the wicked temptation of doing what he wanted.

"Kansas," he admonished. "Don't you trust me?"

"Not for a single second." Or herself either, but she didn't say that.

"So, I guess this is good-night, then, is that what you're telling me?"

"I'm afraid so."

"Now that's a shame," he said, shaking his head up at the gables.

Kansas slipped out of his grip and unlocked her door.

He came to stand in front of her, bracing a hand on the doorjamb. "Well, nothin' I can do about it if that's how you want things," he said. Then he grinned. "If you're sure that's how you want things."

She was sure that *wasn't* how she wanted things. Just as sure as she was that it was how things needed to be.

"Good night, Linc."

He made a rueful little clicking sound out of the corner of his mouth. "Good night, Kansas."

He pushed off the jamb and turned to go, but stopped before he got too far and faced her again.

Kansas looked up at him, expecting him to say something more. But instead, all at once he took her by the shoulders and lowered his mouth to hers.

It was a friendly kiss at first, not exactly a kiss between friends, but not a passion-filled one, either. But it didn't stay that way for long, as his lips parted wide over hers, pressing her head back into his waiting hand while his other arm went around her shoulders and held her tightly to him.

Kansas's willpower was in short supply by then and resistance was impossible to come by.

Instead, her hands crept to the hard bulges of his biceps, to his broad shoulders, and then one went on its own all the way to his neck—first the sinewy side and then around to his nape where his hair was coarse, just slightly wavy, and felt like heaven.

She kissed him back as if she'd been doing it forever, as if she knew just when to part her own lips in answer to his, when to meet the tip of his tongue with the tip of hers, when to concede to the deepening pressure that pushed her head even further back into his big, capable hand.

Her only misjudgment was in waiting for him to send his tongue courting fully, because it never came. Instead, it was as if he'd only introduced it to her, but stopped short of plundering her with it.

Go ahead. Please, she silently willed, though she wasn't brave enough to do anything that might encourage it. But she wanted it. She definitely wanted it. And more.

Then, just as the craving grew fierce, he ended the kiss altogether.

Kansas opened her eyes to him. His were still closed; his expression was part pleasure, part pain, as if it hurt to stop where he had. He took a deep breath, held it, and then sighed and let her go, not opening his eyes until he'd stepped back.

When he did, that cornflower-blue gaze held her as surely as his arms had, but he didn't say anything.

He only smiled a little ruefully, raised a hand and gave her a small wave before he took the porch steps two at a time in a slightly bowlegged swagger and disappeared into the shadows of the night, as if a moment's hesitation might have kept him from leaving at all.

And there Kansas stood, on her pristine porch, soundly kissed, watching him go, wondering what it might have been like if she had thrown caution to the wind and asked him in after all....

And thinking that her sister and his brother could be wrong.

That it just could be that he was more saint than anyone imagined.

And she was more sinner....

Chapter Five

There was talk about Kansas and Linc the next day. Kansas overheard some of it, pieced together some of it through subtle and unsubtle questions and comments from customers in the store, and listened to a lot of it repeated by Della on the phone that afternoon.

"Yes, he had his arm around me as we walked down the street," she admitted to her sister when Della was finished relaying the rumors. "But no, his hands were not all over me, he did not sweep me up into his arms or carry me to my door. We said good-night on the porch, he did not come in and he did not do rebel yells down the street when he left. We aren't engaged. He didn't try to talk me into running off with him like Virgie did, and he hasn't given me the impression that he's using me to soothe the open wound of his loss. That sounds like a line from a song—it had to have come from Emma Hawkins, bless her ninety-year-old soul. And he isn't sweet-talking me so he can *dump* Danny on me and disappear—that one is so viperous it has to be from Melanie Mason." Kansas sighed. "Did I leave anything out?"

"He loved you all along, married Virgie to keep from doing wrong to a mere twelve-year-old, and now that Virgie is gone and you're grown up, he's come back for you."

"Stella Magraw," Kansas pegged the originator of that bit of fiction. "Lord, you don't think she'll try to sell it to one of those tabloid newspapers the way she did that theory that the new barber was really Elvis moved into Elk Creek to hide out, do you?"

"Anything is possible."

Kansas let her forehead fall to her hand. "Good grief."

"You definitely brightened up the coffee talk today."

Kansas cringed. "I know," she answered ruefully, hating it.

"What do you want for yourself, Kansas?" Della asked then, out of the blue and sounding sad and confused herself.

"You know the answer to that." And Kansas knew what her sister was afraid of.

"I'm not sure I do. If you could pick your future out of a catalog, what would it be?"

"Pretty much the same life you have. I'd marry a nice man, have kids—" She stumbled over those words but then said, "You know."

"Would you stay in Elk Creek to do it?"

"Of course. There's nothing for you to worry about, Della. I'm not leaving here. Ever. I realize you feel like I'm really the only one of the family that you

have in your life, now that Mama and Daddy have left
and gotten so busy with their retirement, but you don't
have to worry about my moving, too, because it isn't
going to happen."

Her sister seemed to ignore this reassurance. Instead, she said, "What kind of a man would you
choose?"

So it wasn't only that Della was fretting over Kansas running off with Linc the way Virgie had. Her sister also wanted to remind her of some things. "You
know the answer to that question, too."

"No, I don't think I know this one at all. I thought
I did, but I don't. I thought that once you got over
John Mitchell and the operation, you might give Dave
Nolan or Sandy Morton a chance. I know they aren't
much to look at or big businessmen, but they're nice
enough fellas who would care for you and treat you
well and give you my kind of life. But you don't want
anything to do with either of them. And there you
were last night, laughing it up with Linc Heller of all
people. I'm beginning to wonder if I know what you
want at all."

Kansas was beginning to wonder herself. About the
unfamiliar feelings she had whenever she was with
Linc, whenever she thought of him. About how little
she seemed to know herself at those same times.

"What would you have with him?" Della went on.
"Virgie never had a home or more than she could
throw in the back of that truck of his to move on to the
next rodeo. She never saw her family—and even if
she'd wanted to, how often would it have been? A few
times a year at best? She'd have never really known my
kids the way you do now. She couldn't have shared
things with us—holidays, birthdays, weddings, the

births of my babies, of hers, nothing. She couldn't have close friends. She couldn't have anything at all but one motel room after another. One long, empty road after another. One strange face after another. She couldn't have anything but Linc Heller."

"And Danny."

"She didn't have Danny for long before the life she led with Linc killed her."

"Car accidents happen everywhere all the time, Della. It didn't have anything to do with the life she lived."

"Didn't it? It happened in the middle of the night on the way from a seedy roadhouse, probably because Linc was driving recklessly."

"We don't know that. We don't know that at all," Kansas repeated what she'd said to Della in the store that first day Linc had come back to town.

"I suppose the next thing you're going to tell me is that he's a changed man. That he isn't the same person who used to guzzle beer every Friday and Saturday night. Or the same one who raced up Center Street at a hundred miles an hour. Or the same one who shot out all the lights in town on graduation night. Or the very reason the city council voted to enact a curfew for teenagers just so everyone could get some peace from his all-night rabble-rousing and ruckus-raising."

"I don't know if he's changed from all of that, Della. But I do know it's possible, because Bucky did every one of those things right along with him—and so did half a dozen of his friends—and Bucky and the rest aren't doing any of it now, are they?"

"Bucky and the rest only followed his lead. And they've all settled down. Linc Heller still traipses all over the country, rootless and irresponsible," Della shot back. "Is that the kind of life you'd want for yourself? Or would it be all right for him to do just what Melanie Mason said—dump Danny on you to raise while he takes off and only drops in when he's passing by to flatter you and coax his way into your bed until he takes off again?"

"No, that wouldn't be all right." And her sister had finally succeeded in reminding Kansas just how crazy she was in losing sight of the vast differences between herself and Linc Heller and the lives they led. "It wouldn't be all right at all."

Della's tone softened again. "I just don't want to see you hurt. I know how you've been feeling since the operation. I know you think you're not much of a woman anymore, though that's just so wrong I want to shake you. And I know that a man like Linc Heller paying attention to you must make you feel whole again. But Kansas, let another man help you heal. A good, stable, steady man who'll stick around to prove he cares for you over and over again, not one who'll take it all away with him and leave you feeling more empty than you did before he came."

Della knew her too well, Kansas thought at that moment. Maybe she knew her better than she knew herself. "You're right," she said quietly, realizing that being with Linc, having his attention, his compliments, did just what her sister said—it made her feel like a woman again. An attractive, desirable, feminine woman. Not just the empty shell of one. And that had enough power all by itself to blind her to the realities of how ill suited she and Linc were.

"Oh, Kansas." Della sighed, sounding frustrated and almost on the verge of tears. "I've wanted a man to come along and show you how wrong you've been

about what that damn operation left you with . . . or
without. But I never dreamed that man would be Linc
Heller. I wanted it to be someone good.''

"Linc isn't bad," she defended, believing it. "But
you're right that we're complete opposites. That we
don't want the same things. It's just hard to remember it sometimes."

"When he's sweet-talking you and looking at you
with those eyes of his like you're the only woman in
the world. I know, I saw how it was last night."

Kansas took a deep breath and straightened her
shoulders. "I just have to stay away from him."

"Far away," Della agreed.

"I'll arrange to spend time with Danny alone. In
fact, how about if I have your kids and Danny for a
sleep-over tomorrow night?"

Della laughed with relief. "You know I never turn
down free baby-sitting. And you're right—see all you
want of Danny, only do it away from Linc."

"That's the best way."

"Absolutely."

So why did it feel so bad?

"Yep. It's Kansas a'right."

"Hey lady, don't you answer your phone or return
messages?"

The sound of both of those voices tickled her senses
in spite of herself as Kansas stood beside her car while
the dockhand at the train station lifted fruit crates into
the back of her station wagon that evening.

She turned in their direction and found Linc and
Danny coming her way.

The tall, broad-shouldered man was dressed in a
body-hugging black T-shirt, tight blue jeans and cow-

boy boots. The tiny boy beside him wore tennis shoes, baggy jeans and a green T-shirt with a Tazmanian devil on the front of it. One look at the two of them and her heart took a leap.

"Hi, Danny," she called, honing all her attention on her nephew.

The boy ran the last distance to her. "We bin callin' you today."

"You have?" she said airily, roughing up his hair and trying not to notice his father's long legs closing the gap to join them.

Courtesy demanded that she finally glance at Linc, but glance was all she did. A brief acknowledgment of his presence so she didn't linger long enough on his sharp-planed face to let him get to her. "Hi," was all she said before pretending to watch what Elmer the dockhand was doing.

"You're a hard woman to get hold of," Linc answered.

"Busy day," she lied. "I was going to call you later to see if Danny can spend tomorrow night at my house. I thought I'd have a sleep-over for all the kids so he can get to know his cousins. Would you like that, Danny?" Once more she stared intently at her nephew.

"Wha's cousins again?" he asked his father, wrinkling his little brow.

"They're the relations that are kids like you," Linc informed him.

"They're anxious to meet you. We'll have a barbecue and roast marshmallows and you can all stay up playing as late as you want," Kansas enticed.

"I has to brin' my blanket," Danny warned solemnly.

"That's all right. Billy is a year older than you are and he has to have his stuffed rabbit to sleep. Even April, who's two years older, will bring her favorite doll, and Nic has a blanket, too—he turned three in February. Only Ashley won't bring anything, but she's seven."

He looked all the way up the long length of his father. "Can I?"

"I don't see why not."

Elmer loaded the last crate and closed the car's rear door. Kansas thanked him and then had to give in to looking at Linc.

His head was bare; his dark, rich, coffee-colored hair was combed neatly, but it bore a faint line that said he'd worn his hat sometime earlier. He was clean shaven and he looked too good to her. Much too good. She knew she had to get away quickly and took her keys out of the pocket of the navy blue slacks she wore to let him know that's what she meant to do.

"I can pick up Danny after I close the store or you can drop him by there earlier or—"

"I'll bring him to your house," Linc said, cutting her off. But before she could escape, he laid an arm across the roof of her car. "I called because Danny and I wanted to treat you to supper tonight. After taking care of us when we were sick, we wanted to do something for you."

"There's no need for that. I was happy to help." Too prim. Lord, but she hated it when she sounded that way. And there he was, smiling at her as if he could see how uncomfortable she was standing right there out in the open with him. She wondered if her being on the lookout for anyone seeing them had alerted him. But whatever it was, he seemed to find the whole thing funny.

"Come on, Kansas, if we made you happy by taking your help, then you make Danny and me happy by letting us buy you supper."

She looked in the car window as if double-checking the crates when in fact she knew very well there were no problems with them. The problem was in how tempted she was to accept Linc's invitation. She countered the temptation with the reminder that his taking her to supper meant eating with him in public and adding fuel to the gossip.

"There's only the two restaurants and they're usually crowded," she hedged. "Besides, I have to get this fruit back to the store and into the cooler anyway, and it really was a long day—"

She stopped talking when he leaned very near to her ear and whispered, "I know what everybody is saying about us."

Another brief glance at him when he straightened showed her that his smile was now a full-blown grin. And that he had wonderful white teeth, laugh lines around his eyes and creases in his cheeks that only made him all the more appealing. As if he needed age—or anything else for that matter—to make him more appealing.

"I don't like to be the subject of talk," she said bluntly. And too primly again, darn it anyway.

"When they're talkin' about you, they're leavin' someone else alone," he joked.

"Doesn't it bother you—the things that are being said?"

He chuckled. "Nope. Couldn't care less. Why should you?"

Kansas thought about that. "I just don't like it," she muttered. But all the while she considered his point of view—what difference did it make if people talked about her? It wasn't as if she'd done something wrong and the talk was exposing it. People just gossiped. Her, included. She wasn't beyond repeating a juicy bit of information to Della when she heard one. Or listening to her sister relate something she'd learned at the beauty shop. It was harmless.

Still, though, she reminded herself somewhat belatedly, she needed to keep her distance from Linc no matter what. "I really do have to get this fruit back to the store."

"Okay. Come with Danny and me to look at the old holding barn, then we'll all go to the store. I'll unload these crates for you, and we'll have supper afterward."

"Please, Kansas?" Danny finally said, after having stood quietly by, watching the two adults. "We wanna eat wis you."

And she wanted to eat with them. Both of them.

She looked directly at Linc then, letting her eyes meet his wonderfully sparkling blue ones for the first time. "I really want to spend time with Danny, get to know him. But is it smart for you and I—"

"It's just supper," he reassured her.

For a moment she wondered if that was what he'd told himself to get him here, too, because it sounded like a rationalization he'd grown comfortable with.

But he was right. It was just supper. With Danny along.

"Why do you need to look at the holding barn?" she asked, to buy herself time to make sure she was doing the right thing.

"It hasn't been used in years and Jackson was wondering if we should sell it or tear it down. He wanted to see what I thought." Linc nodded in the direction of the fruit crates. "Besides, those things must be heavy. You'd better let me unload them for you. I wouldn't want you to strain anything important."

She didn't tell him she didn't have anything important to strain. Instead she stared at Danny while the familiar wave of regret washed through her. "So you want to take me to supper, do you?" she asked the little boy.

"Yep, I really do," he answered her with such gallantry it touched her and made her want to laugh at the same time. How could she resist?

"Okay then."

"It is all right if I come along, too, though, isn't it?" Linc added.

Kansas held her hand out to Danny. "What do you think? Shall we let him?" she asked as he took it.

"Course," he answered. "He has to cut my meat."

Kansas did laugh at that, and the laughter eased some of the tension she'd felt.

"I'll cut yours, too, if you let me," Linc said, making it sound lascivious.

"I'll just bet you would," she countered. Then she said, "Well, if we're going to the barn first, we'd better do it. This fruit will spoil if it sits out too long."

The holding barn was directly across the street from the train station, so they just walked over. Not only had it not been used in years, it hadn't had anything done in the way of upkeep or repair, either, and the football-field-size building was becoming an eyesore. There were those citizens of Elk Creek who argued that it gave a poor first impression to anyone arriving by train. There were others more concerned with staying on the good side of the Hellers, who said it was far enough at one end of town not to be a factor, since most people drove in anyway.

To Kansas it had a certain old-fashioned charm, with its high, sloped roof, its cross-buck great doors and the railed cattle pens that ran alongside. But it was run-down. The rail was broken in places and hadn't been whitewashed in years. The red paint on the side walls had turned to umber and peeled. The roof had holes in it.

Linc unlocked the padlock on one of the great doors and flung them wide. The flutter of birds' wings greeted them as several escaped from nests in the rafters through the weather-ravaged roof.

"Jackson wasn't kidding when he said it had been a long time since this place was used," Linc observed as he led the way inside.

In its day it had been not only a place to house cattle waiting to be shipped to market, but also the site of a number of auctions of prime breeding stock. There were few divisions of space—some stalls at one end, and a raised, railed platform near the center that had served as an auctioning block, as well as a place to stand to oversee the cattle when the place was full. There was a loft covering half of the rafters, but for the most part, the barn was just a big, dirt-floored empty space that showed Kansas the reason some townsfolk wanted it torn down.

Somehow, though, as she went from looking around the place to watching Linc, she had the impression he was seeing more than she was.

Danny ran off to the end where the stalls were, climbed onto a gate and rode it open like an old hand. The hinges squeaked and so did something else—no doubt a rodent occupant Kansas didn't want to think about. She did, however, climb the four steps to the platform that seemed somehow cleaner with a bright ray of sunshine beaming down on it through a missing section of roof.

Linc's thumbs were hooked into the corners of his pockets as long, slow strides took him looking around, checking out what there was to check out.

And from her perch, Kansas had a bird's-eye view of him.

Why did the man have to be so attractive? Even his few flaws were sexy. It was as if sensuality just came out of his pores naturally. And Kansas was not immune. If wishing made it so, she would have been, but she wasn't. One look at him and all her senses kicked into overdrive.

So don't look at him, she ordered herself, forcing her gaze to the rafters.

"This barn has definitely lived past its prime," she said.

"Oh, I don't know," Linc mused. "I've seen a few places like this given new life."

"As bird sanctuaries?"

He looked at her from where he stood just below, judging the platform. "Use your imagination, Kansas," he challenged.

She kicked at a dusty web in the lower corner of the railing. "A spider preserve?"

"I was in an old barn in Nebraska that had been turned into a wholesale furniture store and another in Oklahoma that had been sectioned off into booths that were rented out to folks to sell whatever they had a mind to try selling—crafts, handmade clothes, gadgets..."

"I don't think Elk Creek is big enough to sustain either of those."

"No, I don't suppose so." He came to stand with one foot on the platform's bottom step, one hand on the railing. "Then again, I've seen a fair share of these old relics turned into honky-tonks. Elk Creek could support one of those."

Kansas wrinkled her nose. "A roadhouse?" she said with the same enthusiasm she might have had if he'd suggested turning it into a brothel.

He laughed at her. "A place to kick up your heels. To meet your friends, take a date, dance and laugh and—"

"Drink and be rowdy and loud and—"

"Kansas," he chastised. "There's nothin' wrong with indulging in a refreshment—in moderation. Or with being rowdy or loud now and again. But that isn't necessarily what I'm proposing here. Elk Creek doesn't even have a movie theater. What harm would there be in a place folks could come after a long week of work to listen to some good music, relax, have a cold drink..." He climbed the steps and held out his arms as if for her to slip into them. "And dance?"

"It would disturb the peace and draw a lot of people from other towns to litter and cause problems and fights, and introduce more liquor and all the trouble that comes with it into the community. Not to mention the bad influence it would have on the kids growing up here."

He scrunched up his face, closed his eyes and shook his head, letting his arms deflate to his sides as he did. "Kansas, Kansas, Kansas."

"I'm just playing devil's advocate. The city council would bring all that up before they'd ever give any kind of permit or license."

"We're only dreamin' here, darlin', not debating."

And Kansas felt very stuffy. "I thought you were supposed to decide if you should tear it down or do something with it. I was just pointing out what you'd face if you tried to do something with it."

He stepped up to her and gave her the once-over then, clearly taking in her buttoned-to-the-throat white blouse and even bending around her to glance at the tight coil of hair pinned at the nape of her neck.

Before she knew he was going to, he reached to it and pulled the pins out so that it fell loosely down her back. While she was still fumbling to catch it, he'd unfastened her collar button with just one hand.

"What are you doing?" she demanded, pressing her fingertips to her newly exposed throat.

But as she did that, his hands went back to her hair, finger-combing it free. Then he assessed his handiwork. "Much better. Now close your eyes."

"Excuse me?"

"Close your eyes." He slid his index fingers gently down her forehead until she had, and then traced a path with them around her ears to rest his hands on either side of her neck. "Picture dark paneled walls and a parquet floor, dim lights, a hand-carved bar, candles on the tables, the smiling faces of folks having fun, a live band... a place where a man can take a pretty woman and hold her sweet, soft body in his arms to guide her along the dance floor..."

Kansas's attention was pulled between the exquisite sensation of his touch and the rich honey of his voice licking its way down her spine. And then one of his arms slipped around her while he captured her right hand in his left. All at once he pulled her in close to him, laid his cheek against hers and gave her no choice but to put her own hand on the solid bulge of his biceps.

"Nothin' at all wrong with a man and a woman dancin' a little cowboy cha-cha..." he whispered into her hair, his breath a warm delight.

He started to hum the tune of a popular new country song that Bucky played a lot on the radio, taking a few tentative steps and then a few more when he realized she knew the dance.

"Why, Kansas, you can cha-cha."

She leaned back a ways to look up at him. "Don't sound so surprised."

He pulled her in close again, propping his chin on top of her head. "That's just one of the things I like about you, darlin'—you always surprise me."

He started to hum again, keeping perfect time as they danced in the warm golden beam of late-day sunshine and kicked up dust motes underfoot. His hand around hers was just gentle enough, just firm enough. The pressure of his arm against her back was strong and confident. His body was big and powerful and yet he moved with grace, gliding as smoothly as if they were on ice.

And somewhere along the way she started to enjoy herself so much she forgot where they were, forgot why she shouldn't be there, why she should ever resist anything that felt so good.

"Yes, sir," he whispered. "Hearts can get stolen on a dance floor."

"Maybe I'd better protect mine," she bantered back.

"Maybe you'd better," he said, but he went on humming and dancing, carrying her along as if they'd been doing this together forever.

Sunshine warmed the air around them and Kansas was more aware of the scent of Linc's after-shave than the smells of the barn. Her eyes drifted shut and in her mind she could see vividly the kind of place he'd described. It didn't look so bad in her fantasy and for a moment she wished it was real because she wanted so much to go on dancing with him, to dance with him again and again, to know that there was somewhere she could always go to be in his arms just the way she was....

Then, all of a sudden she came to her senses and pushed away from him, abruptly ending what she was liking much to much.

Linc just laughed at her retreat, bowing low over his arm like an old-fashioned gentleman thanking her for the dance and making her laugh at him in return.

Then he straightened and just when she expected him to tease her about her skittishness, he said, "What do you think? Shouldn't we get that fruit of yours to the store?"

Kansas had completely forgotten about that and even after he said it, it took her a moment to rise out of the myriad of feelings alive in her to remember herself and her responsibilities. "Oh, the fruit!" she repeated when she did, making him grin again.

His sparkling eyes stayed on her but he called, "Come on, Danny. We're done here. Let's go."

And Kansas led the way out at quite a clip.

Danny rode with her and it gave her time to refocus on her nephew. But it was short-lived. When they reached the store he wandered inside and left her alone with Linc again.

Rather than watch him lift and carry the crates into the cooler, she did equal work, trying not to notice the way the muscles in his arms and shoulders bulged as he stacked and carried two crates at once.

When they were finished, she went into the bathroom and took a comb and pins from her purse to fix her hair again.

"Leave it," he ordered, leaning against the jamb where she'd left the door open. "It shines like silk when it's loose. Don't truss it up."

Her hands stopped midway in indecision. Pleasing this man was not something she should be doing.

As if he knew she was torn, he stepped behind her and took the brush from her, running it with slow, steady strokes through the tangles he'd left.

The bathroom was small for two of them to fit, he had to be close enough that she could feel the heat of him, though he didn't touch her with anything except the hairbrush. But she wanted him to. She wanted to settle back into him, to lay her head on his chest, to have his arms close around her, to give her body over to him in the way it craved. . . .

"Okay, okay! I'll leave it down!" she conceded, snatching the brush from him to do it herself.

But he didn't leave the bathroom. He only took the one step backward that he could, crossed his arms over his chest and leaned against the wall, watching her.

Kansas saw him in the mirror, smiling a smile that was impossible to decipher. A few quick swipes of the brush and she jammed it back into her purse. "I'm starved," she announced with vigor, leaving him behind in the bathroom as she rushed out.

Once more he called to Danny, though his voice was a slow drawl, not the urgent, flustered tone of Kansas's, and they left the store.

Kansas insisted on driving herself to the restaurant and again her nephew rode with her. It was easier to remember to concentrate on Danny through the meal they shared at Margie Wilson's café because Kansas was intensely aware that all eyes in the place were on their table.

It was after dark by the time they left the restaurant. They took Danny next door for ice cream for dessert, and the little boy proved he was tired when they were finished and he threw a tantrum over Linc trying to wipe his face.

Kansas watched as Linc reacted firmly but patiently, sending the boy to the truck ahead of him once he'd accomplished the task.

"We'll follow you home," he said then.

"No, go on to the ranch. Danny is worn out and it isn't as if I haven't gone home alone a gazillion times before."

"We Heller men see our dates to their front doors," he told her with mock solemnity, turning her by the shoulders to her car. "We'll be right behind you."

Kansas would have put up more of a fuss, but the mayor and his wife walked by just then, staring openly at them. Instead she said hello and just got into her car.

She told herself on the way home that Linc would only make sure she got there safe and sound, and then go on to the ranch to get Danny to bed. In fact, if she hurried, she could probably put her car in the garage and merely wave to him as she slipped in her front door.

But that wasn't how it worked.

Linc was out of his truck when she'd closed the garage door and he reached her porch at the same moment she did.

Danny seemed to have disappeared.

Linc nodded over his shoulder at the truck as if he'd read her thoughts. "Danny lay down on the seat, stuck his thumb in his mouth and went to sleep."

"You should get him home to bed," she said, giving in to the urge to go to the truck to peek at the boy.

He looked like a tiny, rosy-cheeked cherub and she reached a hand through the open window to smooth his hair from his brow, trying hard not to wish he were hers, a weakness she had with most kids, but one she didn't know if she'd ever conquer. Then she faced the house again without moving from the side of the truck, hoping Linc might get the hint and leave before any more of her defenses dropped tonight.

But he was leaning his shoulder against a porch pole, his thumbs hooked in his pockets again, one ankle crossed over the other and the toe of that boot propped like an arrow pointed to earth, staring at her. "Come on up and sit on the swing with me," he invited. "It's been more years than I want to count since I got to spend a few minutes in the evening breeze on a front porch."

"Maybe just a few minutes," she heard herself say, traitor that her mouth could be lately.

By the time she reached the house, he was in the wicker swing, patting the flowered cushion beside him.

Kansas didn't join him there, though. Instead she curved an arm around the pole he'd abandoned and pivoted until she could prop a hip on the railing that faced him.

Linc chuckled a little. "I won't bite," he said. "Unless you want me to."

There were way too many things she wanted him to do with that devil's temptation of a mouth of his. But she tried not to think about them. "So what will you tell Jackson about the barn?"

"That I danced in the dust with a beautiful woman and could have gone on dancin' until I got myself into trouble?"

"You know what I mean." But what did he mean about getting himself into trouble?

He answered her question instead of enlightening her. "Seems like a shame to sell it or tear it down when it could be put to good use to liven up this sleepy ol' town."

"And who would fix it up and run it?" she challenged so as not to sound as prim as she had when they'd discussed this earlier.

"Details, details, details," he said with a laugh. "Maybe I'll do it when I retire," he finished so off-handedly she knew he was only teasing.

For a moment she just watched him swinging, his arms stretched wide along the top of the seat back, one booted foot resting on the opposite knee. He was the picture of a man at ease on a lazy spring night, dusted with what moonlight could reach under the roof.

He watched her in return, and although she couldn't see more than the shadows of his eyes, she could feel their gaze and she knew he wasn't missing a thing.

"Where'd you learn to dance like we did tonight, Kansas?" he asked then.

She poked her chin his way. "What do you think I've been doing all these years? Living in a box?"

His teeth flashed in a grin. "Lordy, but I love it when you get your back up. What I really want to know is whose arms you were in when you learned."

"Delbert Delvechio."

That made him laugh full out. "How can anyone named Delbert or Delvechio have taught you the cowboy cha-cha?"

"He was the best dancer at the University of Wyoming."

"Ah. You learned in college. Did you button up your shirt collars and pin back your hair then, too?"

As a matter of fact she had, but she wasn't going to admit it. "I happen to like my hair back and my shirt collars buttoned."

"That's a shame," he said through another laugh.

Kansas picked a pansy from the flower box that lined the rail and threw it at him.

He gently took it off his chest and smelled it. "Then again," he mused, staring intently at her again, "I like the idea that you let your hair down and open that button only for me."

There was that intimate tone of voice licking its way down her spine once more. "*I* didn't let my hair down or open my collar, if you'll recall."

The grin returned. "No, I did," he said, sounding pleased with himself. "But you let 'em stay that way."

No denying that. "Shouldn't you get Danny home to bed?"

"What're you afraid of, Kansas?"

"Nothing."

"Sometimes I think that chin of yours might stab right through me. What're you afraid of, Kansas?"

"I'm not afraid of anything." *Liar.* "You and I are just...well, I just don't know what you want with me."

"And you're scared it isn't something you can give."

She knew he didn't have any way to know how right he was. Or how much it hurt. "We're different people, you and I."

He nodded, slowly, almost in time to the back-and-forth sway of the swing. "I'll bet you can give me a hatful of other reasons, too."

"All of them valid."

"Mmm." He studied her for a moment, very solemnly. "I can give you some, too. I've given them to myself often enough since I walked into your store that first day back in town."

"But here you are." She'd meant to say, *then why don't you stay away and leave me in peace,* but that wasn't what came out.

"Yep. Here I am. And there you are, way over there, hugging that pole as if you need protection again. What if I were to walk across this porch, whisk you up into my arms and carry you away to places you've never seen and things you've never done before?"

She might love it. But she wouldn't want anyone to know. And that was the moment she realized there really was a part of herself she hadn't known existed. A part that might be just a little like Virgie after all.

Nothing could have surprised Kansas more.

But it was only a tiny, secret part she'd never act on, so she said, "I guess I'd have to have you arrested and charged with kidnapping."

He laughed one more time, as if she delighted him. He also left the swing to stand very near her, one hand above her head on the pole she hugged. "Then what if I was just to dance with you again right here and now until I'd stolen your heart?"

She might love that, too. But she wouldn't want anyone to know that, either. Or to see it.

Then again, maybe no one would see it. After all, it was late; none of her neighbors were out and in the shadows of the porch she and Linc were probably almost invisible. . . .

"Just what makes you think you could steal my heart?" she challenged.

He laid his index finger against her chin. "Tryin' to stab me again, aren't you?" Then he bent very close to her ear and whispered, "What makes you think I couldn't? Or do you have it buttoned up tight, too?"

"I don't know why you'd want it."

He reared back and looked at her as if she were out of her mind, taking with him the scent of his aftershave, the warmth of his body, and some of the electricity he ignited in her by just being near.

"Any man would want to steal your heart. Do you honestly not realize that?"

No man would want it when they knew just what an empty package they'd be getting, she thought. But she glanced over her shoulder at his truck and said, "It's getting chilly. Danny is liable to catch a cold sleeping out here."

Linc didn't say anything for the longest time, until finally Kansas had to look back at him.

He shook his head. "I'll bet you don't know what a heart stealer you can be, either."

That made her laugh, a shade nervously. "Oh, I have a whole drawerful upstairs. Why, I'm notorious for it around here."

At the edge of the porch where they were, she could see more of his face, and she watched his expression turn into a serious frown. "Well, take mine out of your drawer and give it back, will you? Cause I'm worried about losin' it to you."

He laid his palm against her cheek and kissed her. A warm, sweet, gentle kiss, the kind a boy might give a girl he'd placed up on a pedestal and was a little afraid of himself.

And then, as quick as that kiss had begun, it was over.

Linc pushed off the pole and hightailed it down the steps to his truck, not looking back even once.

And leaving Kansas as surprised as she was confused.

Chapter Six

nsas was ready for her guests when the first wave
ved the next evening. Della's four kids stampeded
the house as if it were their own, calling for her as
y came.

"Hugs," she demanded in greeting, hunkering
wn on her heels and holding out her arms.

Her nieces and nephews charged her, nearly knock-
g her over and making them all laugh. Then, at their
ther's instruction, they went out to the backyard
l Kansas stood to face her sister's frown.

She didn't need an explanation. "I only had supper
th Linc last night. In public. And it was with Danny
ore than with Linc."

Della merely looked at her and Kansas could tell her
ter knew that for the lie it was.

"Oh, Della, don't begrudge me a little weakness."

"Honey, I don't begrudge you a single thing," Della answered from the heart. "I'm just afraid for you."

"Well, you shouldn't be. Nothing is going on. A little flirting maybe, but only harmless flirting." Wasn't it?

Clearly Della didn't believe it was. "I heard you looked like you'd just gotten out of bed—your hair was down, your blouse was open...."

Now that kind of talk Kansas *did* resent. "Melanie Mason again. She is such a witch."

"Is it true?"

"I had certainly not just gotten out of bed! I left the store, met Linc and Danny at the train station when I picked up the fruit, had supper with them—"

"At Margie Wilson's café—"

"And that was it." Or at least all she was admitting to for the moment.

"With your hair down and your shirt open?" Della persisted ominously.

"My hair was brushed out and my collar button was undone. So what? Yours are that way right now, do they mean something?"

"It's just not like you."

"Maybe it's time some things about me changed. Or maybe it's more like me than anyone knows—me included."

"Why are you yelling?"

"I'm sorry. I didn't realize I was," she said an octave lower. "Do you want a glass of ice tea?"

Della shook her head and leaned against the back of the navy-blue-plaid wing chair that angled away from the small foyer into the living room. "I can't stay. Bucky is cooking a romantic dinner for us and you know how he is—he's likely to burn down the house in a fit of culinary creativity."

Kansas picked up the overnight bag her sister had brought in. "The kids' things?" she asked even though she knew very well and didn't wait for an answer. "I draped blankets in the guest room so it looks like a tent and they can pretend they're camping. I thought they'd all get a kick out of that."

Della nodded distractedly, ignoring her sister's attempt to change the subject. "Bucky says I should leave you alone about Linc. He says you're a big girl, that you know what you're doing, and so what if you have a little...fun...with Linc, that I'm making a mountain out of a molehill and if it was anyone else in the world I'd be glad you were dating again, that that's really all you *are* doing."

Kansas didn't know what to say to any of that. It wasn't a perception even she had used in thinking about her relationship with Linc. But it made sense. Why was seeing Linc or having supper with him or sitting on her porch with him any different than doing those things with Dave Nolan or Sandy Morton? Except that she enjoyed Linc's company and didn't enjoy that of the Dairy King manager or the gas station attendant.

"Bucky is right," Della said then. "It's none of my business, and I'm being as bad as Mama and Daddy were about Linc and Virgie. You know what's best for yourself and anything...and anybody...you want, is what I want for you."

"There's no need to be so serious, Del," Kansas cajoled.

"Just promise me you'll be careful."

"I'm the most careful person in Elk Creek," she said with a laugh.

"I know you are." Except Della's tone was dubious. "I'm not going to say another word against Linc. Whatever happens, whatever you start up with him, you're still my sister and I love you, and I'm with you all the way."

"Well, thanks," Kansas answered somewhat forlornly, because Della seemed to believe there was more going on between Kansas and Linc than Kansas thought.

And yet, as she walked her sister out to her car, Kansas felt something of a burden lifted from her shoulders to have Della's reluctant approval.

The trouble was, a sense of freedom to get involved with Linc was the last thing she needed.

Linc wasn't exactly sure just what the hell he was doing as he showered and shaved before taking Danny to Kansas's house.

Or, for that matter, what the hell he was doing courting her the way he had been.

Everything Kansas had said the night before was right. They were very different people who led very different lives. More different than any two people he could name.

And Linc didn't begin to understand why what had happened between them happened at all.

But Lord, just one look at her and things popped and sizzled inside him. One thought of her and his nerve endings rose to the surface of his skin. And that wasn't all that rose....

He was a pretty disciplined person, for the most part. He worked out even when he didn't want to. He rarely even had a beer anymore. He'd never smoked more than an occasional cigar. He didn't stay out all night partying the way he used to. And when he set his mind to something—or to staying away from something—he'd never had trouble following through with it.

Until now.

No matter how much he told himself to stay away from Kansas, he couldn't seem to do it. It was as if some stronger force drew him to her.

And he was tired of trying to fight it. And failing.

What was the point, anyway? Was it going to hurt anyone if he and Kansas spent a little time together? Even if he couldn't control staying away from her, he could control what came of it. Like the night before—he'd hardly kissed her. If he could keep up that way...

But could he?

He splashed after-shave on his face and the sting of it helped him steer away from thoughts of what else he wanted to do with Kansas.

He had to try resisting at least that part of the attraction.

"So here's the deal," he told his reflection in the mirror, leaning in close as if to convince himself he meant business. "You can look, but you can't touch. That way neither of us gets in too deep and we don't get hurt."

But even though he was determined, it worried him that he was tempting fate to see her.

Because he wanted her in the worst way.

Danny was riding his father's hip when Kansas answered her front door and found the two of them on the other side of the screen. The little boy's green eyes were wide over the thumb that was in his mouth and the index finger that rubbed a corner of his blanket against the tip of his nose. His other arm was wrung around Linc's neck as if he were hanging on for dear life.

"We're feeling shy about meeting the cousins," Linc informed her when she pushed open the screen for them and he stepped inside.

"Oh, you'll love them, Danny. They're kids just like you," Kansas assured him, rubbing his tiny back. Then she held out her arms and said, "Come on and let me show you."

Danny tightened his neck-hold and laid his head against his father's.

"I think I'd better take him to meet them and stick around until he warms up some."

"Sure," Kansas agreed, though she'd hoped Linc would only drop Danny off and leave before he had time to make her pulse quicken. But it was already too late for that anyway. One look at his broad shoulders in the chambray shirt he wore and his narrow hips in those tight jeans was enough to double her heart rate. "The kids are in the backyard playing with clay. Just let me set Danny's bag in the bedroom and I'll show you the way."

It didn't help matters at all that her hand brushed Linc's when she took the backpack from him. Or that she could feel his gaze on her back—and lower—when she led him down the hall that ran alongside the stairs, through the kitchen and out to the yard.

Huge oak trees shaded the picnic table that was in the middle of the lawn near a brick barbecue pit. There was a card table set up not far from it with an assortment of tubs of Play-Doh on it and several gadgets that fashioned it into a variety of shapes and objects.

"Look, Aunt Kansas, I'm making purple spaghetti this time," a little girl in pigtails and a pink romper called.

"Just don't eat it again," Kansas said. Then, to Danny, "That's your cousin April."

"She gotth a boo boo," offered the little dark-haired boy beside her who was just Danny's size.

"That's Nic. He already turned three but not very long ago," Kansas explained. "How did you get hurt, April?"

But it was Nic who answered, "She thlid off the thlide too fatht and thcraped her bottom."

April pushed him for revealing that and he shoved her back.

"Come on, guys, don't fight," Kansas said. She moved to stand behind the oldest girl, a round-faced child with eyes so dark they were nearly black. "This is your cousin Ashley."

Ashley barely looked up from the hamburger she was fashioning, intent and serious in her work and unimpressed with yet another kid younger than she.

Then Kansas reached across the table and poked the ribs of the pudgy four-year-old who stood staring at Linc, his mouth open in awe. "And that's Billy."

"My dad says yer a real cowboy what rides buckin' broncos."

"Yep, he is," Danny answered proudly, taking his thumb out of his mouth and straightening up but keeping a possessive arm around his father's neck.

"Wow," Billy said, drawing the word out into a sigh.

"Yep," Danny answered, making Linc and Kansas both chuckle at the solemnity between the two small boys.

Linc ruffled Billy's hair affectionately but spoke to Danny. "Wouldn't you like to play with some of this stuff?"

"You play, too," his son demanded, making it clear it was the only condition under which he'd consider it.

"Maybe for a little while," Linc answered, setting Danny down at the free spot at the table and kneeling beside him.

Billy promptly came to Linc's side to demonstrate how to mold monsters, obviously intent on impressing him.

"I think I'll get supper started," Kansas announced.

"Can my dad stay, too?" Danny asked instantly.

"The boy takes coaching well," Linc said with a laugh.

But Kansas could tell the request had originated with Danny alone. There was too much honest anxiety in it. She could hardly deny him.

"Of course he can stay, too," she assured, having some trouble pulling her eyes away from Linc's lopsided grin. "If he doesn't mind eating hot dogs."

"Don't mind at all," he answered. "If you don't mind having me."

No, that wasn't what she was feeling. "You're welcome," was all she said.

By the time Kansas had gathered all she needed from the kitchen and had the hot dogs on the grill, Linc was sculpting horses out of pink clay while a rapt audience of five watched, each of them demanding one of their own. And she realized that whether it was good for her or not, Linc had become a part of this party.

The kids enjoyed his company through dinner as much as Kansas did. Ashley, who fancied herself all grown-up, seemed to have developed a crush on him and took it upon herself to wait on him like a hand-maiden. Clearly his charm wasn't lost on little girls any more than it was on big ones, but seeing the care he took with her niece's feelings only endeared him to Kansas.

For dessert they roasted marshmallows and crushed them along with chocolate bars between graham crackers. It was Danny's first taste of s'mores, and he ate three before his father stopped him. The littlest Heller was back to being himself and joining in as if he'd been a member of the group his whole life at that point, but no one—especially not Kansas—was anx-ious to remind Linc his presence among them was no longer needed.

After they'd all eaten, Nic started a round of beg-ging for horseback rides from his aunt. It was dusk by then but Kansas, accustomed to this request, got down on all fours anyway. Linc joined in. Billy and Danny wanted their horse to buck and then so did the rest of the kids. Linc obliged, and, not to be outdone, so did Kansas, who had a great time at it until she was ready to drop from exhaustion, which was what she did, rolling to her back on the grass. Nic took that as an invitation and pounced on her, and within seconds she was wrestling with all five giggling imps.

"I give up! I give up!" she finally called through her own laughter, only to collapse once more and find Linc standing above her, clearly enjoying the scene.

He shook his head and said in an intimate tone, "Yep, you always do surprise me, darlin'."

"*Darling!*" Ashley repeated in a voice full of scandal and secret delight before giggling even harder than before.

Linc picked the little girl up and flung her over his shoulder, threatening to toss her into the trash and delighting her further still.

The sun had completely set by that time and the air was cool. Kansas called for all the kids to go in, put on their pajamas and get ready to watch the movie she'd rented for them.

They protested until she said she'd turned the guest room into a tent and then they were all excited enough about seeing it to comply.

And suddenly Kansas was alone in the quiet of the night with Linc.

His hands went to his hips, his feet were astride and he leaned his weight on just one leg, grinning from ear to ear. "Well, aren't you a sight."

Kansas reached for her hair, knowing even before her hands touched it that the lacy elastic ruffle that had held it in a ponytail at her nape had slipped down and left the thick mass loose and fluffy. She pulled it free, bent over at the waist and gathered the strands at her crown, where she used the ruffle to make a Gibson-girl knot rather than let him think she'd leave it unfettered to please him.

"Danny seems to have settled in," she said when she was finished.

"Are you askin' me to go?"

"No..." Just thinking that she'd be better off if he did.

"Good, because I couldn't leave you with this mess and face myself in the mirror." He turned to the card table and started to close clay containers. Kansas had no choice but to get busy on the supper things.

"You're pretty kid-smart," he said as they worked. "The barbecue, the s'mores, the clay, making a tent to lure them inside when the time came, getting a movie so they'll wind down and more than likely fall asleep before they know it . . . I'm impressed."

"It's all fun for me."

"I saw that."

Kansas realized suddenly that her madras shirt had come untucked from her cutoff jean shorts. She poked it back into her waistband.

Linc had stacked the clay tubs and toys, and lined his horse sculptures in a row. With no more to do, he joined her at the picnic table, helping there, too. "Would you consider fixing up a birthday party for Danny?" he asked then. "He's getting old enough to need one and I don't know where to start. Not that you have to," he added in a hurry. "But if you wouldn't mind and it wouldn't be too much trouble . . ."

Kansas couldn't keep from smiling at him. "I'd love to," she said, meaning it.

"Nothing too big or fancy, just a little something like this, out at the ranch. I'll pay for it all and do whatever you tell me to help—"

That made her laugh. "When have you ever done what anybody told you?"

He grinned again, but only with one side of his mouth. "Now?"

She considered testing him by telling him to go home because she was having too good a time with him. But she was afraid he might. Instead she picked up all she could carry and headed for the house. "I'd love to give Danny his first birthday party," she repeated.

Linc gathered up nearly all of what was left and followed her inside.

The sound of the kids' rambunctious voices came from the bedroom. Kansas set everything down and said, "I'll get their movie started," leaving Linc there.

When she got back, he was rinsing dishes and putting them into the dishwasher.

He didn't hear her return, and for a moment she stood in the doorway watching him. He dwarfed the counter, and his big hands looked almost comically oversized handling the small juice glasses the kids had used. But there was something very pleasing about the sight. And taking in the vision he presented from behind stirred up other emotions in her, as well.

Kansas hurried past him and went outside for the last few picnic remnants, willing the cooler air to calm her senses.

It helped only for as long as she was gone, stirring up all over again just as soon as she went in and caught sight of his gorgeously rugged profile.

"So what I don't understand, Kansas," he said as he conceded the sink to her at her insistence, and leaned his hips against the counter facing her, "is why a woman who's as crazy about kids as you are isn't married with a bunch of her own."

She considered a glib answer but then something inside urged her to scare him off with the truth. "I was engaged. In fact, I would have been married for eleven months now. To a man named John Mitchell. He came to Elk Creek a few years ago, taught fourth grade—at least until the breakup, then he moved away."

"What happened?"

"The wedding was all set, preparations were under way, and I started having some female problems. Went to the doctor and discovered that I had tumors that had strangled my ovaries. I had to go in and have a hysterectomy—they cleaned me out completely," she ended, trying to make a little joke, but her voice cracked and gave her away.

"You can't have kids," Linc nearly whispered, as if he knew what a blow it was to her.

Kansas closed her eyes for a moment, fighting tears that had come from nowhere and had no business being there. When she could, she said, "Things with John changed after that. He tried to put a good face on it, but he turned sort of aloof and he lost his enthusiasm for the wedding. He kept suggesting we put it off, even though physically I was fine after recovering from the surgery. I knew he loved kids as much as I did. We'd talked about having four—like Della and Bucky—and, well, I finally had to offer him his ring back in place of the babies I couldn't give him."

"Ah, Kansas," Linc nearly groaned, his sympathy echoing in his voice. "And he took it?"

"Gratefully. Not that you could blame him."

"Like hell."

That made her laugh and eased some of the tension.

"You're better off without a guy like that. Besides, if he was here right now, I wouldn't be and I wouldn't like that a whole lot."

She gave him a sidelong look meant to chastise him but caught sight of herself in the darkened window over the sink and realized it looked more come-hither.

Finished with the cleanup, she turned off the water with great finality. "I'd better check on the kids."

Linc followed behind and they found all five of them asleep in various odd places. Kansas turned off the movie and they carefully repositioned and carried small sleep-heavy children until they were all tucked into the two double beds. Then they slipped out of the room and Kansas waited expectantly for Linc to go.

Instead he pointed his chin toward the rear of the house, patting his back pocket as he did. "I must have dropped my wallet on the lawn when we were playing horse with the kids. Come help me find it."

She could hardly deny him that so she followed him outside, wondering as she went how she could feel so comfortable with him and so fired up by him at the same time, and trying to unhook her eyes from those two empty jeans pockets he'd mentioned.

The glow of the porch light didn't reach as far into the yard as they'd been and the night was cloudy enough to block any light from the moon. When they got to the spot they needed, they had to search on all fours the way they'd been before.

"Here it is," Linc said when he located the wallet, holding it up in a victory salute. But once he'd replaced it in his pocket, he sat on the grass, one leg bent at the knee, one arm balanced on top of it, clearly in no hurry to get up and leave.

Once more Kansas's only option was to join him, sitting cross-legged on the lawn, as far away from him as she could get without making it obvious—which wasn't anywhere near as far away as she should have been.

He just happened to be facing the house and for a moment he stared at it, causing Kansas to glance over her shoulder to see if there was any particular reason. There didn't seem to be.

"I like your place," he said then, as if he knew what she was thinking.

"It's nothing special."

"You've made it special—warm and cozy and comfortable and inviting . . ."

"Careful, talk like that could ruin your image."

"Oh, it's worse than that. I enjoyed this whole night—the barbecuing, playing with the kids, even doing the dishes. And then there was last night, sitting on your porch—I liked that, too."

Kansas went from staring at the house to staring at him. "That's an odd thing to hear from a person who chose to leave all that behind for a life of traveling around."

"It's an odd thing for me to find myself feeling."

"Does that and coming back to Elk Creek to set up housekeeping have something to do with Shag's passing after all? I mean maybe now that he's gone, you don't have anything to prove by running off and living a wild life."

"Actually you're right about part of that—the not-having-to-prove-anything-anymore part. But not about the timing. It wasn't Shag's death that did it. It was birth—Danny's. There was something about having him that made me start to understand my own father. A little, anyway. And that made me grow up. Finally Shag's disapproval didn't get my back up the way it had before. I knew I could take care of my family and all of a sudden I knew I wanted to do it in Elk Creek, whether Shag was here or not."

"That was when you decided you and Virgie should come back," she guessed. "You started to tell me about that the first night, when you were sick and I was making orange juice," she prompted, curious about the details he'd been too ill to go into then.

But Linc didn't say a word.

Even in the shadows cast by the trees she could see his square brow all beetled up.

She forged ahead in spite of it. "Was Virgie looking forward to finally coming home, too?"

After another moment's silence he said, "I'd answer that question but I don't think you'd believe me."

"Why wouldn't I?"

"For the same reason you don't believe I can appreciate your house or enjoy a night like this one or the last."

"But here you are proving me wrong," she challenged. "So maybe I might just believe whatever you say."

He seemed to consider whether or not he was going to enlighten her. But when the silence between them stretched on and Kansas began to think he was deciding against it, she said, "Tell me about my sister."

He breathed a wry sort of chuckle, shaking his head. "I don't really have to tell you about her. She hadn't changed from when she was a girl here. She liked being rowdy and shaking things up, having a good time. She was restless and she had more energy than two people. Being pregnant nearly killed her just because she had to take it easy, couldn't barrel race or... party... the way she liked."

What had he stumbled over saying? Was *party* another word for drink? Virgie had liked to do too much of that even before she'd left Elk Creek.

And what did it mean that he sounded so weary, or maybe even disgusted, when he said it? "She must have loved Danny," Kansas said, feeling the inexplicable need to defend her sister.

"She did. She loved him more than I'd ever seen her care for anything or anyone—me included."

"But she didn't want to bring him back here?"

Again Linc hesitated before answering, sounding reluctant when he did. "No, she didn't want to come back to Elk Creek. Or settle anywhere else, for that matter. She was happy following the circuit, moving around, seeing the country, even when it was country she'd seen before."

"But what about Danny? Surely she wanted what was best for him?"

"She didn't see any harm in his always moving around."

"But you did?"

Linc yanked a handful of grass from the ground and tossed it away with some force. "Maybe we shouldn't talk about this."

"I'd like to know."

The strength in her voice brought his face toward her again. He stared at her for a while, as if judging whether or not she really meant that. Or was he wondering if he should really tell her? Then he took a deep breath and sighed it out, staring at the house again.

"Virgie and I had a difference of opinion," he said quietly and very solemnly. "I wanted to come back here and make a home for us, a place where she and Danny could stay put, where I'd travel from."

"And Virgie didn't want that?"

"She wanted to go on barrel racing, traveling, she wanted everything just the way it was before she got pregnant." His voice dwindled off and for a time he seemed lost in the memory.

Then he shook his head and went on. "But we had this new baby and I thought he needed a stable home to grow up in and...well, I just hated to see him carted around from town to town. We could live on my earnings if she was in one place with him, but we couldn't live on hers if I was, so she just seemed like the one who should keep the home fires burning." His voice turned very, very quiet. "We were arguing it when the accident happened."

That sounded like a confession. "Was the accident caused by the argument?"

He looked her in the eye. "Are you sure you want to hear about this?"

"I'm sure."

Still he seemed reluctant and didn't jump right in. Finally he sighed and said, "It was our first night out after Danny was born. We left him with some friends, went out to supper, to a movie, and then Virgie wanted to go to a honky-tonk outside of town. I'd broken my ankle a few weeks earlier and couldn't dance, but she wanted to go anyway—to listen to the music, she said. And she was driving because I couldn't, so that's where we ended up. It was good, though. Some of our friends were there and Virgie got to dance after all. Then I thought we ought to get back—"

He shook his head. "I should have left her alone. She was having a fine old time, and she'd been cooped up for so long with the end of the pregnancy and Danny's birth and then having a new baby to take care of. I should have just let her enjoy herself as long as she wanted. But I didn't. She got mad, said I was trying to tie her up. We started to fight and pretty soon we were arguing about her settling down, coming back to Elk Creek, the whole thing. In the heat of it she was driving a lot faster than the speed limit and she missed a curve in the road..."

"Virgie was driving when the accident happened?"

Linc frowned over at her. "You didn't know that?"

"We just got word that the two of you had been in a wreck, that you were in a coma, but Virgie had been killed instantly, that the baby hadn't been in the car at the time and was all right. We were all so stunned—learning that Virgie was dead, that she had a baby...and then there were all the arrangements to bring her home to be buried, since no one knew how long you'd be in a coma..."

"It must have been a mess."

"Virgie was driving," she repeated to herself.

"You all thought I was," he guessed.

"Yes, we did."

"And blamed me for killing her."

"I wouldn't say that exactly," Kansas hedged.

But Linc wasn't fooled. "That explains some of why Della looks at me the way she does. She thinks I lured Virgie away from her family and caused her death, doesn't she?"

"I know no one needed to lure Virgie out of Elk Creek—she'd have left no matter what. But we all thought the end was different."

This time when he looked at her, his eyes bored into her. "I would never have willingly done anything to hurt Virgie."

Kansas nodded her acceptance of that. Funny, but somewhere over the years she'd pictured Virgie growing up and calming down. She'd imagined her changed from the way she'd been as a girl. She'd come to believe in a fantasy of her not too different from Della's, though she hadn't realized it until now.

And she liked that vision of her sister better. Because what Linc had described was the Virgie she'd known before and it made her sad to think that her sister hadn't really matured at all, that she'd have put satisfying her own restless spirit before the welfare of her son.

"Virgie always had a wild streak a mile wide," she admitted. "If she hadn't changed, then she wouldn't have been happy staying at home, even with a baby she loved. Especially not while you went off without her." But a part of Kansas understood, because while she wouldn't want to be as rootless as her sister had been, she also knew she wouldn't want to be left behind alone while any husband of hers traipsed all over.

It served as a reminder to her to put some distance between herself and Linc, which she did by shifting positions to lean on her hand, angling her feet out to her side, between them.

"So why didn't you bring Danny back to Elk Creek yourself after the accident?" she asked then.

"I came out of that coma to monumental medical bills. Everything I'd saved to come here and set up housekeeping went to the hospital, and even that didn't make a dent. I couldn't have left Danny in Elk Creek without asking for help—mostly from Shag— and I wouldn't do that. So Danny and I hit the road again until I'd earned enough in prize money to pay off my debts. I'd done that and had enough left over to do what I'd intended before. We were headed here when Jackson tracked us down to tell us Shag had passed on.''

Linc picked a single blade of grass this time, leaned forward and circled her anklebone with it. ''But we're here now and glad of it,'' he finished in a lighter tone.

Kansas was staring at him as the moon broke through the clouds to shower milky light on them. It struck her all over again how handsome he was, with his thick, dark hair and the sharp planes of his face and even the small scar to the right of his forehead that showed silver.

He was staring back at her, holding her with his eyes and smiling a soft smile that said they'd both seen hard times but emerged intact to go on with their lives.

And she wondered how it was that he could reach right to her heart without even touching her.

''It's getting late,'' she said suddenly.

His smile turned knowing, but he ignored what she'd said. ''You made me jealous watching you wrestle around in the grass with the kids—all free and easy and just like one of them,'' he responded instead.

''I was only playing with them.''

He rolled onto his hands and knees the way they'd both been before, putting his face not far from hers, close enough that she could see the glint of mischief in his eyes. ''Seeing you like that gave me a glimpse of a side of you I think you hide deep down. Made me want a closer look.''

''That's one of the joys of kids—they give you a chance to be one again with them. For a little while,'' she said, fighting the urge to rear back, because she knew he'd tease her if she did.

"That doesn't need to be the only way it happens. Playful can be good even between people who've grown up. How come no man ever taught you that, Kansas?"

"Who says they didn't?"

He chuckled. "That chin'll tell on you ever time."

She finally did lean away from him, though she couldn't go far. "Don't be silly." *And don't look at me that way and raise gooseflesh on my arms.*

"Silly's just what I want to be after all this serious talk tonight. Silly and maybe just a little bad."

"I suppose you think you're going to get my goat with the insinuation in that, but it won't work."

"Your goat isn't what I want, darlin'."

"What do you want?"

"You." He leaned far enough over to catch her mouth with his in a kiss that toyed with her.

"You're crazy," she said when it was over.

"Okay."

Before she had any idea what he intended, he grabbed both of her ankles and pulled them out from under her, leaving her lying on her back in the grass with him on all fours, straddling her.

"Oh, Lord, Mavis next door will see this from her kitchen window and blow it all out of proportion and spread the story by dawn," she whispered urgently.

"She'll say we were makin' love right in the yard. Naked as jaybirds," Linc whispered back, laughing and clearly enjoying himself. "But that isn't what we're doing. We're just lookin' at the stars."

"We are not."

"Okay."

He captured her mouth with his once again, only there was very little about it that was playful now, and much that was pure, raw sensuality as his lips opened over hers and he lowered his body to lie beside her, one thigh across her lap.

He caressed the side of her neck inside her shirt collar and moved that leg against her ever so slightly, setting off sparks inside her.

She tried to tell him to stop, but it only came out a moan of pleasure as his tongue flicked against her lips and teased the tips of her teeth just before introducing itself to her tongue in an erotic, inviting dance too delicious to resist.

Kansas didn't know when it had happened, but somewhere along the way her hands had tangled themselves in his hair and the feel of his head against her palms was arousing all on its own.

Stop this, she told herself.

But she just plain didn't want to.

He slipped his arms underneath her and pulled her against his unyielding chest, holding her so tight she thought she could feel the racing of his heart. Or maybe it was her own.

The thought of the neighbors' watching eyes flitted briefly through her mind, but she couldn't seem to care about anything but having that kiss go on and on, about the heat of Linc's body infusing hers, about the leg that still wrapped her and the hardness of Linc pressed to her.

Her shirt came untucked again with little effort and his hands found their way under it to her bare back. Shards of white light shot through her at that first contact of skin against skin and she wished suddenly that she'd been liberated enough to go braless.

But it didn't matter. Linc made quick work of the hooks and one hand began a slow slide around to the front of her. Slow enough to let her know she could stop him if she wanted to.

But she didn't. In fact she only wished he'd speed it up.

When he finally reached her breast and covered it with that big, powerful, callused hand of his, the feeling was so exquisite her back arched all on its own and a small groan escaped her throat. Bliss. It was pure, unadulterated bliss.

Still he kissed her, plundering her mouth while his hand worked such magic at her breast, kneading, exploring, teasing her nipple to a hard, straining crown and sending bolts of lightning in a straight shot that set off a whole new craving between her legs.

Then he tore his lips from hers to kiss the bare skin of her side, nudging her shirt out of his way and freeing her breast to cool night air for only a moment before the warmth of his mouth covered the very crest.

The glory of that drew her back into an even deeper arch. She wanted him to make love to her. Conservative Kansas Daye wanted to be naked as a jaybird and making love right there on the grass of her backyard.

And the shock of realizing that gave her a sudden burst of control.

"No more," she said, part groan, part command.

Linc stopped, but slowly, nearly weakening her will before he let her go completely.

"You do things to me that I don't understand," he said in a passion-raspy voice.

"Well, fight it," she ordered almost comically, though she still wanted him too much to laugh. She put her clothes aright and once more groaned, though this time in agony. "Oh, Linc, we should just stay away from each other."

"I can do a lot of things. But that isn't one of them." He got up, reached for her hands and brought her to her feet, too. "And I don't want to," he added, looking into her eyes for a moment before he kissed her again, lightly. "And you don't want to, either."

No, she didn't.

"So what are we going to do?" she whispered.

"I guess we're just going to see each other, give in a little to whatever this is that's pulling us together and go wherever it takes us."

"Oh, I don't know if that's a good idea," she hedged, because she knew very well where she wanted it to take her—where it very nearly had just now.

"Sometimes you just have to ride with it, darlin'," he advised.

Then he kissed her yet again, softly, lingeringly, but holding back just a little something that made Kansas want him all the more.

"Good night," he whispered, striding steadfastly to her fence, where he high-kicked his way over it to disappear into the shadows that led to the front of her house.

And Kansas was shocked at herself all over again as she realized that seeing him and giving in to whatever it was that was pulling them together, going wherever it took her, was just what she was going to do.

Everything else be damned.

Chapter Seven

Kansas was up long before the kids the next morning. It was Memorial Day—a holiday Elk Creek celebrated as the kickoff to summer.

She'd already arranged to take her nieces and nephews to the opening parade, planning to meet up afterward with Della and Bucky, who were to ride on the float for the radio station. Linc had said he'd find her during the parade to take Danny off her hands.

Though she didn't want to admit it, it was the idea of seeing Linc today that spurred her to wash her hair at dawn so it could air-dry and be fluffy enough to catch in her rosebud barrette only loosely a few inches from the ends—a compromise of sorts, as it wouldn't be hanging free but it wasn't all tied up the way she usually wore it, either.

She baked two pans of brownies—one for the picnic supper she'd share with Della's family and another to be sold at the church booth. Then she cleaned out a small cooler where ice would keep the fruit salad and pop cold—also her contributions to the evening meal.

When all of that was ready, she set the table for breakfast and made up pancake batter. With nothing more to do in the kitchen and the kids still sound asleep, she took a bath, applied a touch of mascara and blush, and then decided to go ahead and get dressed.

She intended to wear a pair of jeans and a T-shirt, but as she stepped into her closet to get them, something else caught her eye—the filmy dress she'd bought over a year ago.

Bought but never wore.

She'd seen the dress in a catalog early in the spring and fallen in love with it. It had a high, stand-up collar, but from there the armholes angled like a halter top, leaving deep wedges of bare shoulders.

The fabric was a diaphanous white, but the gossamer lining kept it from being see-through. It fit like a glove, with princess seams that shaped it along the lines of her body to midthigh where the skirt flared and whispered to just a few inches above her ankles.

It was the most feminine, romantic dress she'd ever seen. The perfect honeymoon dress, she'd thought, and paid an outrageous price to have it.

But of course there hadn't been a honeymoon.

Della had tried to persuade her to wear it to the Fourth-of-July festivities last year—another celebration Elk Creek did up in fine style—but Kansas couldn't bring herself to do it. John had been gone by then and she hadn't felt woman enough to wear it.

But today that dress seemed to call to her the way it had from the pages of the catalog.

And Kansas threw caution to the wind and put it on.

The parade was as unstructured as it could be, with anyone who wanted to walk along welcome to do it. It began at the train station, traveled the length of Center Street and would end at the park square in front of the courthouse. There booths were set up, games and competitions would be waged, a talent show would be given, and later on, a local band would play and there would be dancing in the pavilion that stood in the center of it all.

Kansas and the kids stood on the sidewalk outside the store and watched as the mayor and his family led the parade, waving from inside his rebuilt Model T. The school band marched and played their loudest, a group of Indians from Cheyenne whooped and twirled and did a native dance in full regalia, the pastor and his wife rode in a convertible, and a flatbed truck conveyed the members of the square dance club as they did a few do-si-dos of their own.

There were as many horseback riders as people in cars or on floats, and a fair share of animals with ribbons tied around their necks being walked and shown off by their owners, young and old alike. There were a pony, three cows, a calf, at least a dozen dogs, two goats, a lamb, a pig, and even a line of ducklings that had bonded to the vet and followed him as if he were their mother.

It was all in a spirit of fun, with the parade participants calling back and forth to the onlookers and some of the onlookers joining in along the way. A lot of the floats tossed candy to the kids and Kansas made sure her charges stayed safe even while trying to catch or gather their share.

Ashley spotted the radio station float from far off and the four little Dennehys started hollering to Della and Bucky long before they could be heard.

Bucky wore a Western suit and a wide-brimmed Stetson with a long peacock feather adding flamboyance to his getup. Della was in a yellow jumper over a white T-shirt, and her smile was as sunshine bright as her dress. She blew her kids kisses as the float neared, but stopped short when she spotted Kansas standing behind them.

"You wore the dress!" she said, and even from the curb Kansas saw tears well up in her sister's eyes.

Kansas just smiled back at her and waved, loving her for caring so much.

And then in the gap left between the radio float and the Retired Citizens of Elk Creek riding a slow-moving, horse-drawn hay wagon, Kansas's gaze was grabbed by Linc, standing directly across the street and staring at her with enough heat to brand her.

She had the overwhelming and inexplicable urge to walk into his arms, but of course she didn't budge.

Instead she watched him peer out from beneath a wide-brimmed cowboy hat to make sure the hay wagon wasn't coming on too fast before he dashed in front of it, light-footing it to her side.

"Why, Kansas, you look good enough to be leading this parade, not watching it," he said in greeting as he unabashedly looked her up and down and bathed her in the warmth of his appreciation.

She hadn't come up with an answer to that when Danny tugged on Linc's pant leg as if it were a bell-pull and Linc picked up his son.

"Lookit I got," the little boy said, displaying his booty in tightly closed fists.

"Two hands full of teeth rotters," Linc answered, his tone admiring and belying his words.

"Yep," Danny countered, accepting his father's awe at face value and adding proudly, "I catched 'em."

"He did," Kansas confirmed. "He's as good at it as the bigger kids."

"That's my boy."

"I got to sleepded in a tent at Aunt Kansas's house and had dinosaur pancakes for bres'fast, too."

"Sounds like you've had quite a time already and here the day is just beginning."

"Yep," Danny agreed, wiggling to be put down. "Gotta go back," he informed him as he rejoined his cousins where they sat on the curb just in front of Kansas.

Kansas glanced back at the parade as the undertaker drove by in the hearse, waving joyfully as he did. But Linc's gaze stayed on her.

"I understand there's to be dancing in the pavilion tonight," he said.

"Oscar Thornbuller's band is playing—The Creek Dawgs, they call themselves."

"Will you go with me?"

"I was going anyway," she said against the rush of excitement his invitation raised in her. "Everybody is."

"Then save me all your dances," he ordered.

Kansas merely smiled.

The end of the parade went past just then. Spectators had fallen in line behind it, walking to the town square and the festivities that awaited there. To the kids' delight, Kansas herded them into the procession and Linc fell into step beside her.

They didn't say much along the way, though. At least not to each other. Linc could easily have been one of the parade's main attractions as people he apparently had yet to see since his return called out greetings, welcomes home, invitations to stop by and congratulations on his rodeoing.

But conversation aside, Kansas was very aware of him.

He wore a bright red Western shirt with mother-of-pearl buttons and the sleeves rolled up to his elbows in that nonchalant way of his. She didn't think she'd ever seen anyone do more justice to a pair of blue jeans—they rode just low enough on his hips, just tight enough around his derriere and thighs to let a person know how great what it all encased was. Even his boots were sexy, she thought, taking in the sharply pointed toes of the silver snakeskin on each cocksure stride.

He'd taken his hat off on the way across the street to her but put it back on as they walked, and although it made him look ruggedly swank, she missed the sight of his dark hair shining like morning sun reflected in a cup of coffee.

Charisma, Kansas decided, the man just had charisma.

And it was her—of all the women he could have—that he seemed determined to spend time with.

Her dress felt better and better.

They met up with Della and Bucky when they reached the park square.

Della hugged Kansas. "You look so beautiful," she said. Then she glanced at Linc, and Kansas wondered if she was only imagining that her sister's expression was softer toward him.

Several of the pets that had been led on parade were gathered on the courthouse lawn and the kids put up a clamor to see them. Bucky persuaded Linc to bring Danny and come with him, and after a moment Kansas and Della were alone.

"I need something cold to drink and a little shade," Della confessed. "Let's buy a soda and go sit on the hill."

The hill was on the west side of the park that sloped down to the sidewalk. The elm trees grew along the ridge and cast shadows that drew people to bypass the old Victorian benches in favor of sitting on the grass.

Kansas and Della did just that when Della had her drink in hand and they'd made their way through the crowd.

From where they sat they could see Linc and Bucky and the kids as the two men stood talking to Rick Meyers, the lumber foreman, and Jerry Clemons, the head of road maintenance.

For a moment Kansas enjoyed the sight of her nieces and nephews with the animals. Danny, especially, seemed to have fallen in love with a little black billy goat that was more interested in chewing his shoelaces than in being kissed on the nose.

Della caught sight of the scene, too, and they both laughed at Danny's attempts at showing his affection.

"He's really a beautiful little boy, isn't he?" Della said, sounding every bit the proud aunt.

"He's well behaved, too. And funny in his so-solemn way—like a miniature Jackson."

"There's not much of Virgie in him, is there?"

"No, not much," Kansas agreed softly, hearing the pain of that statement in her sister's voice.

They fell silent then and Kansas's gaze just naturally went to Linc. He seemed to be telling a story, poking his hat farther to the back of his head with a thumb and grinning from ear to ear until he had the other men laughing uproariously. Something about just the sight of him made her smile.

"He's the reason for this, isn't he?" Della said, catching her at it.

"Who's the reason for what?" Kansas pretended ignorance.

Della pointed her chin across the street. "Linc's attention made you feel good enough to wear the dress."

Kansas hadn't thought of it quite like that. She'd tried to convince herself she wasn't wearing it *for* him, even though she knew she was. But it hadn't occurred to her that he'd changed the way she felt about herself and so precipitated her wearing the dress in that way.

But when she considered it, she realized Della was right. She was feeling better about herself than she had in a long, long time.

"I guess maybe so," was all she said to her sister.

"I'll forgive him a lot for that," Della said quietly.

"There isn't anything to forgive him for," Kansas ventured a little cautiously because she didn't want to renew her sister's hard feelings for Linc.

"Isn't there?" Della asked skeptically.

Kansas weighed her words but relayed what Linc had told her the night before about Virgie, the disagreement over Danny and a stable home, and the circumstances that had caused their sister's fatal accident.

"Do you think he was telling the truth?" Della asked when she'd finished.

"What do you think?" Kansas said, hoping a less defensive tack on her part might work better. Then she added, "We could call for a copy of the accident report. I'm sure it would list the driver. But yes, I had the feeling he was telling the truth."

For a long moment Della didn't say anything at all. She just sat there, staring at Linc.

Then, when Kansas was braced for her sister's usual opinion of Linc and Virgie and the accident, Della said, "I suppose the story makes sense. It sounds like the Virgie we knew, doesn't it? Wild, hell-bent, self-indulgent."

"That's what I was thinking, yes."

"I guess I just wanted to believe she'd grown up. But if she hadn't, she'd have never been happy sitting at home with a baby while her husband traveled around. She just wasn't that kind." Della shook her head as she went on, "There's no denying her temper, either. She wouldn't have liked him taking her away from a good time that night, baby or no baby. And here he is—back in Elk Creek the way he said he wanted to be, taking care of that boy as well as any man I've seen. It lends credence we can't really deny, can we?"

None of what Della said was easy for her and Kansas knew it, so she didn't jump in with her agreement.

After a moment Della turned away from her study of Linc and looked at Kansas. "But what about you?"

"What about me?"

"You and Linc. You care, don't you?"

"I care about him, sure," she hedged.

"And for him, too."

"You think I'm falling in love with him?" Kansas asked with a laugh at the very idea.

"Actually, I didn't think it had gone far enough to be falling in love with him, yet. But are you?"

"Oh, Della," Kansas said as if her sister were having pipe dreams.

"You're showing all the signs. Your eyes are all over him every time he's anywhere around. He can persuade you to do things you've set your mind against— like spending time with him. And..." Della paused, scrutinizing Kansas with a frown. "And there's something different about you since he got to town— even before the dress."

Her sister was right about that—there *was* something different about her lately. She felt freer. More alive. A little daring. Things she didn't know she had in her but was pleasantly surprised to discover, as if Linc brought out the best in her.

"I think maybe you are falling in love with him," Della added.

But before Kansas could even think what to say, the kids, Linc and Bucky rejoined them, announcing plans for turkey legs for lunch.

And Linc and Danny just seemed to be a natural part of the group, gravitating to Kansas as if they belonged to her.

Jackson joined them at midafternoon when his stint running the Cattleman's Association's string-tie booth was over. He'd always been on friendly terms with Bucky and the Daye sisters, talking whenever they met, being on the same committees with them at various times. But he'd never been a part of their group on occasions such as this, the way he was now.

Danny was the common bond. Jackson's affection for his nephew was evident as he hoisted the little boy to his hip to say hello. From there it was just assumed that Linc's brother would go along when the adults took the kids to compete in the games. He was even as loud as everyone else in cheering them on, and did his part in the piggyback obstacle course that required a man with a child on his shoulders to run the gamut.

When that was finished, the men disappeared to the shade around the beer truck to quench their thirsts, and Kansas and Della took all five kids to have their faces painted like clowns.

By the time they came back, Mary Sue Parker and Karen Kramer were using all of their feminine wiles to recruit Linc and Jackson to judge the bake-off. It was clearly an excuse to flirt and lure the two bachelors away.

Coming upon the scene, Kansas suffered a sharp pang of possessive jealousy to see Mary Sue smiling coyly at Linc. She didn't do anything about it, though. Instead she helped Della comfort poor old married Bucky, who'd been overlooked.

But all the while she kept one ear trained on the other conversation so that she knew very well when Linc and Jackson fended off the advances and Linc came up behind her.

"Thrown to the wolves. How's that for you, Bucky?" he complained to his friend. "I'm being eaten alive by a man-hungry female and does your sister-in-law come to my rescue as only another woman could? No, she stands here talking to you."

Kansas glanced at him over her shoulder. "I thought you could take care of yourself," she countered, meaning it to sound glib but hearing the tinge of jealousy in her voice.

"There's that chin again," he said with a laugh, pushing against it with his thumb. "Those eyes of yours wouldn't be a shade greener than usual, would they now? Because that'd make it worth my close encounter with those two man-eaters."

Kansas stared pointedly at her sister. "Did you ever see an ego this big?"

"Never," Della answered, as deadpan as Kansas had been.

Linc's arm came around Kansas's neck from behind, pulling her against him in a careful choke hold so he could say into her ear, "It's even bigger than you think. I told old Mary Sue I'd been laid claim to by the storekeeper."

The innuendo in that made Bucky laugh out loud and Kansas blush, even while his attention warmed her from the inside out.

The older kids began begging to go to the activities provided in the booths set up on the school grounds then, but Danny and Nic wanted to go listen to the children's singer whose music was drifting to them from the bandstand near the pavilion.

Linc suggested that he and Kansas take the youngest two to hear the singer and save them all a spot for their picnic supper while Jackson, Della and Bucky took the older kids where they wanted to go.

Kansas might have had something to say about it had she been able to think. But her mind was trained on the tingling sensation of still having Linc's arm around her, his hand on her bare shoulder. So instead she just went along with the plan.

She had claimed a perfect spot under the biggest elm in the park by the time Linc had retrieved a blanket and cooler from his truck. The tree's giant roots swelled in arcs from the ground and Kansas spread the blanket in the cove of two of them. She and Linc settled with their backs against the trunk as if sitting side by side in a huge armchair.

Danny promptly climbed onto his father's lap, following the curve of Linc's body as if it were a lounger. Nic cuddled next to Kansas and used her thigh as a pillow, snuggling in closer when she began to smooth his hair in a soothing, repetitive caress. Clearly the day had worn out the two smallest children.

The music was singsongy and not at all engaging to adults. As Kansas sat there, she felt her own early-morning and active day catch up with her. She rested her head against the tree and let her eyes drift closed as she sank into the oddest fantasy of herself and Linc and the two boys as a family, all sitting there together close and comfortable and connected . . .

The next thing she knew, Ashley's voice said, "Aunt Kansas is sleeping on Linc!"

And she was, too. Partially. Her head had somehow gotten to his shoulder.

"Shh—let her sleep," Linc whispered.

But it was too late. Kansas opened her eyes and sat up to find the three other kids, Della, Bucky and Jackson all gathered round.

"I should never have sat down," she said in a hurry, embarrassed but at the same time craving to be back where she'd been moments before. "How long was I asleep?" she asked Linc.

He smiled a warm smile. "Not nearly long enough."

The kids jumped onto the blanket then, Danny and Nic roused from their own rests, and Kansas was spared any more comment on the subject.

Supper took them into dusk and as they cleaned the debris, the band started to set up. There were a lot of children in the park, and Della's brood and Danny went off to play not far from the bandstand while the adults mingled and talked to the folks they hadn't met earlier in the day.

Then over the microphone came a loud, "Hee-yaw! Happy Memorial Day to everybody out there!" and the initial strains of music sounded.

From nowhere, Dave Nolan appeared at Kansas's elbow asking for the first dance.

"Not on your life!" Linc called from where he was talking to Bob and Carol Smith, the town electrician and his wife. He cut the conversation short and stepped to Kansas's other side. "She promised it to me. And all the rest after, too."

Dave Nolan accepted that with a nod and a shrug, disappearing the same way he'd come.

Kansas looked up at Linc's handsome face and raised an eyebrow at him. "I don't recall promising you a thing."

He grabbed her hand and pulled her along to the pavilion anyway. "You were talkin' in your sleep at the time, darlin', but it counts just the same."

He took her up the six steps to the whitewashed pavilion with its wooden floor and the low railing that wrapped its octagonal shape and made it look like a giant gazebo.

The Creek Dawgs were a country band and they started off with a rousing song. Linc swirled Kansas into a fast swing dance, clearly trusting that she could keep up after the cha-cha they'd shared in the old holding barn.

She'd barely caught her breath when the next song picked up where the other had left off and Linc had her in his arms again.

"I told you every dance was mine," he reminded, pulling her in close enough to press his cheek to hers.

As the evening wore on there were only two times Linc conceded to Kansas dancing with another man— once with Bucky and once, very late, with Jackson.

Dancing with the older of the Heller brothers, Kansas couldn't help thinking that he seemed different than she'd ever known him to be, as if being around Linc loosened him up, too.

It was an effect Linc had on a lot of people, she realized as she glanced over and was amazed to find he'd persuaded Della to dance with him. There was that way about him that made people feel as if he liked them so much they could let down their guard with him.

Certainly Kansas had let down her guard.

Was it possible she was falling in love with him? she wondered, thinking about her earlier conversation with her sister as she watched Linc over Jackson's shoulder during their slow, silent two-step.

It was more than possible, she admitted to herself. It was likely.

That worried her, for nothing else had changed— they were still two drastically different people with drastically different life-styles.

"Never knew what a good dancer you were, Kansas," Jackson said in his deep, solemn voice, reminding her of whom she was being led around the floor by.

She thanked him, returned the compliment, and in the process, looked up at him with a new perspective, comparing him to his brother.

Jackson was every bit as handsome as Linc, every bit as well built, as much a man. He could be just as charming, though in his own quiet, courtly way. He was hardworking, respected, down-to-earth. The kind of cowboy old Western movies portrayed—a serious man of few words and a strong code of honor who had a gentle side, too, a side she'd seen in his responses to Danny.

And he lived her same kind of life.

So if she was going to fall in love with one of the Heller men, why not Jackson?

But there she was, in his arms, feeling nothing at all.

In fact, it occurred to her that she could be standing in front of a mirror, looking at her male counterpart. It was Jackson's seriousness and down-to-earth quality that made him pale in her eyes, because he was so much like Kansas herself. He didn't set off sparks the way his brother did. Those sparks that lit up the part of herself she had only learned existed since Linc came back. Sparks that made her pulse race, her skin tingle, her senses sizzle. Sparks that reminded her she was alive and kicking and maybe not willing to be just a spinster aunt after all.

But where could any relationship with Linc end up?

Not where she wanted it to, she reminded herself.

And yet, maybe where it ended was less important than the trip to get there, than enjoying the trip and letting it show her the way to being a woman again. Maybe that was worth any ending.

The music stopped and so did the dancers—far fewer of them than had started out, as more and more had left for home with each passing hour. The lead singer announced that the next song would be the last, but still half the people in the pavilion wandered down the six steps to the park.

Bucky had all the kids rounded up and waited on the sidelines for Della. Ordinarily Kansas would have offered to take her nieces and nephews to the car so Bucky and her sister could have the last dance. But tonight she didn't do that. Tonight the last dance was hers.

There hadn't been anything said to that effect, she just knew it and so rejected Della's offer of a ride home and bade good-night to her family as Linc arranged for his brother to take Danny home to bed, too.

Della cast them both a concerned glance but left without a word. Jackson carried off a weary Danny, and Linc turned to Kansas.

He stepped up to face her, smiled a quiet smile for her alone, opened his arms and said, "Just one more, darlin'."

The soft, lilting notes of a slow waltz began, played by a single fiddle as the rest of the band packed up. And Kansas glided into those waiting arms she never seemed to get enough of.

There were half a dozen other couples on the floor, but Kansas was barely aware of them. Instead she let Linc hold her so close it was almost indecent, succumbing to the urge to lay her head in the hollow of his shoulder that seemed carved out especially for her.

He pressed his cheek to her temple and that was how they danced, her soft curves giving way to his honed muscles, the warmth of his breath in her hair, the beat of his heart against her breast, the very faint lingering of his after-shave mingling with the equally light scent of her perfume.

If there was a heaven, Kansas thought, surely this was it.

She wanted the dance to last forever, but she refused to let the fact that it wouldn't mar the moment. And in that, she realized she was willing to do the same with her involvement with Linc.

When the music ended, the fiddler said, "Night, folks," in a bedroom voice.

Kansas and Linc stopped dancing but were a pulse slower in letting go of each other.

"I'm parked halfway between here and your place, but the night is so beautiful what do you say we just walk all the way home? Or are you too tired out?"

He was right, the night was beautiful, the temperature was perfect—just cool enough. The sky was clear and glittered with stars, the air was redolent with the smell of summer just beginning. And a walk home in it meant a few minutes longer with Linc than if he drove.

"I'm not too tired if you're not."

They left the pavilion, Linc with his signature hop-step down the stairs. At the bottom he threw his arms wide as if to embrace the whole world and took a deep breath before letting out a rebel yell. "Ooo-eee, what a night!"

Kansas just laughed at him before he caught her up in a bear hug and swept her right off her feet. When he put her down again he kept one arm around her shoulders and tucked her in close as they headed in the direction of her house.

For a block or so neither of them said anything, settling into their shared gait, enjoying what was left of the evening in companionable silence. Then Linc chuckled a little to himself.

"What?" Kansas asked.

"I was just remembering my first glimpse of you this morning. I could have sworn the sun shone down on you alone, you looked so good."

"You mean for once there wasn't anything you'd loosen up?"

He glanced down at her, taking in her dress. "No, ma'am, not a thing," he answered with enthusiasm. "Today I wanted to tie you up tight to keep you to myself."

"You pretty much did," she reminded.

"Did I ruin your time? Were you dyin' to dance with Dave Nolan after all or that other skinny man I scared away?"

"No," she admitted.

"And how about now? Would you rather one of them was walking you home?"

"Are you just trying to get me to say something to inflate that ego of yours?"

"Yep. But it has to be the truth."

"The truth is, I had a wonderful day and night."

"With me," he prompted.

"With you."

He grinned, satisfied, and tipped his head back to stare at the stars. "There's something happening here, Kansas."

She knew he didn't mean in the sky.

"Something serious," he added.

"I know," she answered so quietly even she barely heard it.

Linc looked down at her again, this time into her eyes, his own conveying his surprise at her easy admission. Very slowly his sensuous lips stretched into an intimate smile. "And you're not even running scared."

"Oh, I'm scared." But she was also excited and thrilled and full of a renewed sense of herself and an overwhelming awareness of this man who had given it all to her.

"Scared in a good way?" he asked.

"I guess so," she said after thinking about it a moment.

"You don't need to be scared at all, you know. I'd never do anything to hurt you," he said as solemnly as Jackson might have as they turned onto her street.

"Sometimes you get hurt anyway," she answered.

"Sometimes you don't."

Neither of them said more as they walked up the center of the road, the only sound that of their steps on the pavement.

But when they reached her yard and headed up the walk to her dark house, Linc said, "I'm feeling things that are bigger than I am."

"Me, too." Once more her voice wasn't much above a whisper.

He chuckled again, almost as softly, and from the corner of her eye she saw him shaking his head in amazement. "There you go, surprising me."

They climbed her porch steps and with each one Kansas's level of anticipation rose, too, though she wasn't sure why. Or maybe she was sure but she was too nervous about what she was considering to face it head-on.

"So, here we are," he said as they reached her door. He let go of her for the first time since they'd left the pavilion and stood back a few inches, as if to give her a little space in which to think.

Kansas lifted a flowerpot full of geraniums off a white wicker plant stand and retrieved her house key.

Linc reached out a long arm and took it from her without touching her. He studied it a moment before the shadows of his eyes swiveled her way and held her. Then he unlocked her door, pressed the key to his lips and handed it back to her, warm from his hand.

Kansas enclosed the key in her fist and swallowed hard over the decision she was making.

"Come in," she said then in a nervous whisper before she hurried inside, as if she weren't sure he really would follow.

And he didn't. Not immediately. And not completely when he finally moved at all. Instead he made it as far as the doorway, letting the screen rest against his back as he leaned a shoulder to the jamb. "Be sure, darlin'. Be real sure."

She wasn't sure of anything except that her heart was racing and desire was a downy thing infusing every inch of her body. But she said, "I am," as if she were.

She sensed in his lingering hesitation that he didn't believe her. But after a moment he pushed off the frame and came inside anyway, closing the door soundlessly behind him. Then he crossed to where she stood in the middle of the entranceway, gently took her hand and led her up the stairs and into her bedroom, where pale moonlight christened the white quilt that covered her four- poster bed.

He went all the way to the side of that bed, just where the moonbeam fell. And there he stood, directly in front of her as if they were about to dance once more.

With a single index finger beneath her chin, he lifted her face to his. "Know one thing, Kansas," he said very seriously, "this is only the beginning, because my heart's involved here."

She couldn't help smiling. "I'll try to be gentle."

That made him laugh. "You do that."

He kissed her then, touching her only with that finger still under her chin and the delicate caress of his mouth over hers. For a man who did everything with such gusto, his caution was achingly sweet.

Slowly he deepened the kiss, parting his lips and merely inviting her to part hers, an invitation Kansas accepted. She let her head fall far back to accept all he gave and finally his arms came around her and closed the gap between them at the same time his tongue made its presence known.

For the longest time that was all he did—kiss her, hold her, almost chastely, until Kansas wanted him so badly she could have cried. Or maybe it was by design, because when he finally lowered the zipper at the back of her dress, she was so eager for more that she forgot to be inhibited and reached for his shirt buttons.

It occurred to her as he shrugged out of it and she got to see his bare chest for the first time just how big a step she was taking with him. But the thought was only fleeting as she feasted on the sight of him. Broad shouldered and well muscled everywhere, he was a magnificent sight. Beautiful really, but in the most masculine of ways.

He slid his hands inside the back of her dress and slipped it forward, off her shoulders to the beginning swell of her breasts, freeing her neck and collarbone to his seeking mouth, nibbling, kissing, flicking the scant tip of his tongue against her skin and leaving a moist trail to air-dry in his wake.

"I'm falling in love with you, Kansas," he whispered against her heated skin. "And I want you so much I'm about to burst."

She could only sigh her answer because by then he'd eased her dress to the crests of her breasts and was working slow magic with his mouth on his way to her straining nipples.

But before he reached them, he abandoned her altogether to pull off his boots and unfasten his belt buckle and the waistband button of his jeans—a second invitation, but this one she didn't think she could accept.

Then he returned to her, kissed her once, quickly, tore back her bedcovers and swept her up into his arms and onto the mattress in one fell swoop.

But he didn't join her there. Instead, from inside that moonbeam still, he grasped both her calves and slid his hands in a slow, steady, forceful downward caress to slip her shoes off and toss them to the floor.

His eyes stayed with hers, hot and intense as she pulled the barrette out of her hair and shook it free, feeling wanton and liking it.

He bent over her and, with his hands on either side of her to brace his weight, recaptured her mouth with his, this time with an urgency that answered what was coiled deep inside of her.

Kansas arched her back to him, surprised at the boldness of her own mouth and tongue in response to him but reveling in it nonetheless.

He pushed himself back up into the moon's caress to take her dress the rest of the way off, and then, shedding all of his own remaining clothes, he finally joined her on the bed, laying that wonderful body beside her.

Oh, but that first contact of his naked flesh to hers was blissful! Warm, masculine skin and the hard length of his arousal molded to her as he finally clasped her breast in a strong hand that was the texture of a well-worn saddle.

Things awakened inside of Kansas that she had never known as he kneaded her burgeoning flesh, fondling her, finding her erect nipple to circle the sensitive outer hues, to roll the crest between his fingers, to make it kernel even more with desire that shot all through her and made her moan deep down in her throat.

His mouth left hers and replaced his hand, suckling, nipping, driving her wilder still. She plunged her fingers into his hair and discovered herself pressing her hip against the evidence of his desire, the part of him she hadn't the courage to explore the way she was tempted to.

And then his hand followed a path down her stomach to her panties, just inside the lace that edged the low waistband, and she remembered the hated scar that was hidden just behind it.

"What's wrong?" Linc asked in a rough, passion-raspy voice, clearly sensing her newborn inhibitions.

"Nothing," she lied.

"Do you want me to stop?"

Did she?

She didn't. She wanted him, wanted to know the weight of his body over hers. Wanted to know the full extent of everything he could do to her. But would it be all right? Would *she* be all right? Or would she disappoint him?

"No, don't stop," she finally managed in a shaky voice. "It's just that . . . since the surgery I haven't . . . maybe I'm no good—"

He stopped her stumbling words with a tender kiss that grew deeper and deeper. Then, with infinite care he kissed his way down the column of her throat, between her breasts, to her navel. He delicately slid her panties down just below the pale scar and kissed it, too.

"It's a terrible shame no one was man enough to give you a baby of your own before it got too late. But there's nothing about you that isn't good. Better than good—glorious."

He rose back up to kiss her again while he divested her of her underwear and started once more to patiently rekindle what had been flaming inside of her before.

It didn't take long. Her heart and senses were full of the wonder of him and her body longed to be, too.

Just as he'd known intuitively her inhibitions before, he seemed to know how much she wanted and needed him inside her now.

He rose above her and, in one fluid motion, slipped into the waiting emptiness as if he were meant to be there. And in the perfection of that act, in the building passion of each thrust, he chased away any lingering doubts she had, taking them both to a climax so spectacular that Kansas cried out and clung to him even as he tensed above her, driving home more deeply than she thought possible and making her feel completely a woman again.

Everything grew still in the aftermath of the moment that suspended time. Their bodies, their breath, their heartbeats. Holding her tight, Linc rolled them both to their sides and settled her cheek against his chest, his hand cupping the back of her head as he pressed a cherishing kiss into her hair.

"I think the falling's over and I'm already in love with you," he whispered softly, his words cradling her heart the way his hand cradled her head.

And as they both drifted to sleep Kansas forgot about there being any differences at all between them.

Chapter Eight

"Wake up, darlin'."

Warm lips pressed to the sensitive junction of Kansas's neck and shoulder. One hand cupped the back of her head; the other kidskin palm traveled a slow path down her bare back and up again. Her naked breasts were against a wall of magnificent masculine chest. And her thigh was in between two much bigger, brawnier ones, prickly with hair.

But even as those facts sifted through Kansas's senses to her brain, she hovered heavily on the edges of sleep, too comfortable, too exhausted to really leave it.

"It's morning, Kansas," Linc's honeyed rasp of a voice said, tinged with a note of urgency. "I didn't mean to sleep this long. We don't want anyone seeing me walk out at this time of day."

That penetrated. Town gossip about having dinner or dancing with him was one thing—it didn't affect how people treated her. But word that Linc Heller had spent the night was something else again.

Kansas's eyes flew open. She raised her head from his chest, and in reflex, her leg rose between his. But the contact with his private parts startled her and she pulled away in a hurry, looking at his face to find him smiling.

"As you can tell, there are definitely better things I could do with this time than slinking off. But I won't."

Sure enough, they'd gone to sleep in the soft, milky glow of moonlight, but it was the first hazy pink of dawn that bathed them now.

Even so, Kansas was torn between instant desire and better judgment.

Lord, but it was glorious to wake up in Linc Heller's strong arms!

The mattress and sheets were like a downy cloud all around them. The air outside of their nest was chilled, but inside it was just warm enough. Naked skin against naked skin in a perfect melding only passion and sleep could accomplish. Her nipples were hard already. His arousal was a long, steely length at her hip...

Resistance was an agony that made Kansas groan. But she said, "You have to go," with the same resolute knowledge he had.

"Come with me."

"With you?" she repeated dimly, frowning her confusion up to his whisker-shadowed face, his hair sleep tousled and wonderful.

"I have to go to Texas today."

"Texas?"

"There's a rodeo and the company I'm signed on with for endorsements has some things scheduled for me. I'll be gone until Friday."

"Danny's birthday."

"Come with me," he said again. "Jackson was going to keep Danny, but we can take him, too. Or we can have just a trip for the two of us."

She could hear the excitement in his voice, the carefree, adventurous side of him that couldn't fathom why such an appealing idea might be rejected.

"Come on, say you'll do it," he coaxed charmingly. Temptingly.

"I can't." She hadn't meant to sound so appalled.

"Why not?" he asked with an underlying note of laughter in his tone, as if he were confident any reason she gave could be surmounted. "You're a free woman. You're over twenty-one. What's stopping you?"

"There's no one to run the store, and I can't just leave it closed. People count on it, count on me—I provide all the staples for Elk Creek."

"Della could open it a few hours a day and Bucky could announce on the radio that everybody'd have to shop then."

"I'd go broke."

"Not in just a few days, you wouldn't."

"I can't do business that way. And there's Danny's birthday party—"

"We'll do it when we get back. He's too little yet to care or know the difference if we have it the day after."

Kansas wasn't comfortable anymore. "I'm not Virgie, Linc," she said very softly, rolling away from him to her back and holding the sheet clenched in two fists above her breasts.

He raised up on his forearm and looked her straight in the eye, his own brow furrowed now. "I know you're not Virgie and I don't expect you to be. I don't *want* you to be. Hell, I was trying to make Virgie into a woman like you."

"What you want me to do is something Virgie would have done. Not something I would."

"I realized I'm in love with you, Kansas—all I had was one single night with you and now I have to up and leave. All I want is to have you with me. To have more of what we had here in this bed, to have some freedom from watching eyes and worrying about waking up in time to sneak out, when what I'm dying to do is make love to you again. That's all. I'm asking for a few days, not for you to be a different person."

"But I'd have to be a different person to give those few days—at least like this, without any preparation or plans or making arrangements for the things I'm responsible for."

His eyes bored into her for a moment before he chuckled a little and shook his head. "I suppose that's true," he conceded. "But if I'd given you some warning, would you come?"

Would she? Would she go traipsing off to a rodeo with him?

Before he'd come back to Elk Creek she'd have scoffed at such an idea. But now? With Linc?

"Maybe," was all she'd commit to.

It made him laugh. "We're going to have to work on that."

"You could stay in Elk Creek," she heard herself say with a challenge of her own, not knowing she was going to say it at all until the words were out.

"No rodeos here this week, darlin'. Though I am going to see what I can do to arrange for the endorsement things to be done closer to home so trips away aren't made any longer than they have to be."

The glibness of that statement brought back to Kansas that no matter how wonderful their night of lovemaking, no matter how strong their feelings for each other, nothing else had really changed.

The sun was getting higher all the time and Linc glanced over his shoulder at it then. "Damn, I have to go."

But he didn't act on it. Instead he laid his palm to her cheek and kissed her—long, lingeringly, deeply. A kiss that chased away those thoughts Kansas didn't want to have in the first place.

She lost herself in his mouth on hers, his lips parted and moist, the heat of his breath against her skin, the rise of his arousal against her side. Her fists opened and let go of the sheet to slide to his shoulders and around to his taut back.

He seemed to take that as an invitation. His hand left her cheek and nudged its way beneath the covers to find her breast. Sweet, delicious sensations awoke at his touch, lazier than they'd been the night before, languorous and lovely, as if they had all day to be sated.

But they didn't have all day and as the sun broke over the horizon Kansas knew it.

She ended the kiss and pulled away from his attempt to start it again. "Linc—"

He kissed her chin and the hollow of her throat, still tantalizing her breast in a way that left her breathless. His only response was a moan that was more pleasure than anything.

"It's getting later," she reminded, weakening with desire.

He pushed the sheet aside and kissed a line to the breast his hand had readied for him, taking the crest fully into his mouth.

Kansas was the one to moan then as white-hot shards of pleasure scattered all through her and brought her back up off the mattress and closer to the source of that bliss.

Maybe the neighbors would sleep late. Or not notice Linc if he left just a little later...

She didn't really care at that moment, as she wrapped a leg around his hip and eased against the straining shaft that let her know he wanted her every bit as much as she wanted—needed—him.

Then, suddenly, he let out a fierce, loud growl and yanked himself from her as forcefully as if someone had done it for him. "I have to get out of here, Kansas, or I'll never go," he said in a harsh, husky voice.

"Never go, then," she heard herself say, once more surprised by her own words.

He kissed her again, a hard, hungry kiss that made her wonder if he might stay after all, forever in her bed, the way she longed for at that moment.

But then he tore himself away a second time. "Come with me," he repeated, sounding desperate for her to do that so they could finish what they'd begun.

And Kansas was more tempted than before by a body crying out for him.

Still she said, "I can't," sounding as if she were in pain, which she very nearly was.

He laughed a little raggedly. "Listen to us. You'd think I was going off to war. I'll only be gone a few days."

A few days too many, Kansas thought, but she said, "Mmm, only a few days."

He stood then and she feasted on his naked derriere, feeling sparks glittering inside her just at the sight and silently willing him to turn around so she could see the front.

But he didn't. Instead he dragged on his jeans and zipped them up, prolonging her torment by leaving the waistband button unfastened as he pulled on his shirt to hang open and untucked.

"Will you look in on Danny for me?"

"No one could keep me away."

"I'll be back by three or four on Friday."

Kansas nodded, watching him rake his long lean hands through his hair and realizing that was all it needed to look good.

"Don't get up. Go on back to sleep," he ordered as he put on his boots, finally buttoned his shirt and jammed the tails into his jeans—a trip Kansas's gaze rode along with.

Then he leaned over her and kissed her one more time, deeply, before pushing himself up again. "Can I call you?"

That made her laugh. After everything else he'd done to her, he was asking permission to call. "Yes."

Belatedly he seemed to see the humor in that, grinning sheepishly. "Will you think about me?"

"Probably." Probably she wouldn't think about anything else.

"I'll think about you. All the time. And wish you were with me." Then he put the tip of a single index finger to his lips, kissed it and pointed it her way. "It's going to be a long few days."

She nodded, suddenly fighting embarrassing tears, for some reason she didn't understand. "Keep safe," she managed.

This time it was Linc who nodded.

And then he left.

Kansas knew it was silly, but in the days that followed, Elk Creek seemed much emptier without Linc. She was as busy as ever and still the time dragged by, dull and dreary.

The weather didn't help. As if the sunshine had gone away with him, dark, heavy clouds settled overhead, drizzling rain and taking away the feeling of summer having arrived at all.

She called Jackson on the first morning Linc was gone, offered to help with Danny and asked if she could have her nephew spend the second night with her. Anticipation of that kept her going until she could drive out to the ranch to pick him up.

The weather was even more dismal by then. The sky was black and overcast, and rain poured in such dense sheets she had to turn on her headlights to see. But as she parked in front of the house, she felt better. Being with any of her nieces and nephews always raised her spirits and Danny gave her a sense of connection with Linc on top of it.

Jackson answered the door and ushered her quickly inside. He immediately took the grocery sack she carried out of her arms, as if he couldn't bear to see a woman carrying anything.

"Those are just a few things for Friday night. I thought I'd save myself having to haul everything out here then. Linc did tell you about Danny's birthday party, didn't he?" she asked a little belatedly.

Jackson nodded, his expression as solemn as a sentry. "He told me."

"And it's okay with you?"

He nodded just once.

"Where is Danny?" she asked then, wiping her feet on the mud mat just inside the door and glancing into the sunken living room where the big-screen television was on.

Jackson motioned with his head in that direction. "We found a station airing Linc's rodeo live. Come on in and sit down. You won't be able to tear that boy away until he sees his daddy's ride."

"Linc will be on TV?" Kansas asked, excitement brewing inside her at just the thought of getting to see him, even like that.

"Next event," Jackson confirmed, waiting courteously for her to precede him into the other room, which Kansas did once she realized that was what he was doing.

She happened to round the couch just as a commercial came on, and she had the sense Danny might not have unglued his eyes from the set to greet her otherwise. As it was, he popped up to his knees, his tiny face showing a similar excitement to what Kansas felt.

"Aunt Kansas! My dad's gonna be ridin' a bunkin' bronc on TV!"

"I know, your Uncle Jackson told me," she answered with a laugh at his enthusiasm and affection for his father.

"Come'n watch wis me," he invited, hitting the cushion next to him and pleasing her no end.

Kansas sat down while Jackson set the bag she'd brought on the dining room table and then rejoined them just about the time the commercials ended. On came a camera shot of the rodeo arena as the voice-over announced the saddle bronc riding event, calling it the cornerstone of rodeo and explaining that it was the way rodeo had all begun.

Kansas's pulse picked up speed even though Linc's name was last on the list of the order in which the contestants would ride.

The living room was dim; the TV screen was so big and the sound so loud that it felt as if they were in the middle of the arena. But as she watched the competition with her silent, rapt companions, her excitement began to turn to tension. Somehow she'd never considered how brutal a sport it was until now, and knowing someone she cared about was on the cusp of participating in it put her on edge.

"There's my dad!" Danny said proudly, in that little-man way he had, when the camera panned to the chutes and caught Linc.

"Yep," Jackson confirmed, somehow managing to convey his own pride in his brother in that single word.

The commentator gave background on Linc, with particular emphasis on his win in Las Vegas as the camera stayed on him. But Linc was the picture of concentration, seeming oblivious to anyone at all watching.

He tugged his hat down tight on his head and then pulled a well-used glove onto his left hand, cinching it to his wrist with a rope wrapped around and around, tied and knotted—the last given an extra yank with his teeth.

Half a dozen cowboys were nearby or perched around the chute, readying the animal the announcer called Tornado. This was Tornado's fifth rodeo; he'd yet to be ridden the full eight seconds, and the fact that Linc had drawn him was clearly the high point of this, the final ride in the final round.

The crowd cheered as Linc climbed over the rail onto the horse's back and adjusted his seat. Obviously he was a favorite, but it seemed as if he couldn't even hear the roar.

Before he had a chance to get completely settled, Tornado reared, catching a handler by surprise and nearly pulling him into the chute. Linc had to grab hold of the side rail to stay in the saddle himself.

"Mean animal," Jackson observed needlessly, while Kansas felt as if her heart were in her throat to realize it herself.

Danny jammed his thumb into his mouth even without his blanket being anywhere in sight, and sucked to beat the band. Seeing it, Kansas moved closer to him and wrapped an arm around him.

"Maybe Danny shouldn't see this," she suggested to Jackson.

"Gotta see my dad," Danny informed her.

"He's seen it before," Jackson added. "But if you don't think you can watch, you're welcome to go into the other room till it's over."

But by then Kansas couldn't *not* watch.

Instead she took a deep breath and stared at the screen again as Linc grasped the rein in his left hand and adjusted things below the side of the chute that the camera couldn't pick up.

And then she heard the same deep, resonant voice that had whispered in her ear as he made love to her two nights before. "Go!"

The gate flew open and Tornado exploded through it, bucking as if his tail were on fire. Linc's right arm was in the air as it had to be, whipping around so fiercely it seemed that it might come loose from the socket.

The horse kicked with deadly intent, its hind legs seeming to barely touch the dirt before leaping into the air again, turning, twisting, giving a punishing, battering ride in answer to Linc spurring him on to worse and worse.

Watching, Kansas thought she could feel every buck of the animal, every slam of Linc's body against the hornless saddle.

How could eight seconds last so long?

She held her breath so she wouldn't cry out the way she wanted to. Agony, it was plain agony to watch. And as much as she wanted it to be over with, she was terrified of what might happen if he let go of that rein and was flung from the saddle.

Finally the buzzer sounded and two pickup men galloped out to either side of the animal—one to grab the rein, the other offering his much calmer horse for Linc to vault over.

He did, landing with a terrible jolt, but on his feet, and the crowd went wild. Even the announcer shouted into the microphone, "Linc Heller rode the Tornado! He rode the eye of the storm and won!"

Jackson gave a huge whoop and shot out of his seat, hollering, "I'll be damned, he did it!" before seeming to remember he wasn't alone.

Danny tore out of her arms and jumped on the couch, mimicking his uncle's yell.

But all Kansas could do was sit like a limp doll and watch as Linc brushed himself off. He swept his hat from his head and ran the back of his forearm across his sweaty brow, grinning ear to ear as he did, pure joy beaming out of his every pore.

He'd loved it, Kansas realized in a way she hadn't when he'd merely explained his feeling about rodeoing to her. He'd taken the worst that animal had to dish out and loved it.

The announcer read off his score and officially proclaimed him the winner, reigniting the cheers from the stands. The camera followed Linc to the sidelines where he was clapped on the back, his hand shaken with vigor, and from out of nowhere a beautiful blonde in skintight jeans and a Western shirt open to an ample cleavage rushed up to him, wrapped her arms around his neck and dragged him into an open-mouthed kiss.

"That's Becca," Danny informed. "Everywhere my dad goes, she fines him."

A rodeo groupie, Kansas thought, feeling the recoil of that kiss in the pit of her stomach even as she watched Linc take the woman's arms down and set her away.

Then, with the crowd still roaring and the commentator still heaping praise on Linc's rides, past and present, commercials played again.

"Well," Kansas said, exhausted, shaken to her toes, unsure what to do about it, and hating that her voice quivered even in the simple word she'd meant as a segue out of the attention they'd all been paying to the television.

"S'all right, Aunt Kansas," Danny soothed, patting her on the back. "You don't has to be a'scared anymore."

Jackson chuckled as if he'd have laughed out loud but was too polite. "You're white as a sheet, Kansas. Would you like a glass of water?"

"No, thanks. I think Danny and I had better just head for my house before the rain gets any worse."

She stood and walked around the couch while her nephew hopped over the back of it and beat her to the door where his backpack waited.

Jackson followed behind, telling Kansas he'd be picking Danny up first thing in the morning because they had a trip to Cheyenne planned. Then he took a big umbrella from the stand beside the door, opened it and walked them all the way to her car, where he protected them from the rain, waiting until her door was closed to wave and go back in the house.

Watching his father's ride had apparently sent adrenaline through Danny because he was more animated on the drive to Kansas's house. Even through supper he chattered about his father. It left the way free for her to subtly ask about the woman he'd called Becca.

"She likes my dad," he answered simply. "But she's not nice as Shelly or Randa. Shelly brin's me snow cones and Randa le's me sit on her horse Tandy."

Kansas felt a wave of that same jealousy she'd experienced when she'd come upon Mary Sue flirting with Linc on Memorial Day. Only this was much more potent. These other women were a part of Linc's life— they no doubt knew him better than she did. And how many of them knew him as intimately?

"Does your dad like them, too?"

"Not Becca. She's silly. Like once time when we got home at night she was waitin' for us in the bed. My dad got maaad at her," Danny said with eyes wide enough to prove just how mad. "He likes other womans though. We take 'em to supper like we taked you."

Oh, the ugly bite of the green-eyed monster!

But rodeo groupies or women who competed or were connected to the festivities were a reality. A part of what Linc's life involved. Of what it would involve whenever he was on the circuit, no matter who he left behind at home.

And that was something she'd do well to remember, she realized as she cleared the table when they were finished eating. Something she'd do well to remember along with so many other things she had a tendency to forget the minute she was with him.

But at that moment any thought of Linc was unsettling, and so she turned her attentions all on Danny and baking cookies together.

She let her nephew make as big a mess as he needed to to participate fully and the results were untasty. But Danny was very proud of them and she didn't let him know that she'd nearly cracked a tooth trying to chew one.

After that they played board games until it was past his bedtime and he was visibly worn-out. Then she gave him a piggyback ride to the guest room to get him dressed for bed. She tucked him in and read to him long enough for him to fall asleep before going to bed herself.

She'd intended to thumb through a magazine but couldn't concentrate and ended up just staring at the foot rail and listening to the storm raging outside.

Where was Linc at that moment? she wondered. Was he with Shelly or Randa? Or even Becca, who he'd be free to join in bed without Danny being along? Or maybe there were others. Surely there were. He was an extremely attractive single man and the evening's hero.

But the worst of what she felt, in spite of knowing better, was just plain loneliness for him herself. And it made her realize, with something of a jolt, how deeply she cared for him.

When the phone on her bedside table rang just then, it startled her. Not wanting to wake Danny, she snatched it out of the cradle before it could sound a second time, her mind running down the list of emergencies that it might be heralding at eleven at night.

But it was Linc's rich mahogany voice that answered her hello.

"Close your eyes," he said right off.

"Excuse me?"

"Close those baby greens of yours. I'm about to tell you what you're missin' and I want you to see it in your mind," he teased.

The sound of his voice washed through her like a gentle ocean wave clearing the shore of debris. All the evening's darker thoughts receded; she rested her head against the headboard and closed her eyes. "Okay, shoot," she said, playing along.

"The company I'm doing endorsements for had my room changed. When I got back tonight a bellboy led me up to the twenty-sixth floor of this hotel to a room fit for royalty. As we speak I am in a bathtub I had to climb three steps to get into, tiled all over—inside and out—in hand-painted porcelain. It's big enough for four people... or for two people to do more than sit and soak. There are flowers all over the back edge that smell like I'm takin' a bath in a garden. I'm in the dark and looking out two cornered walls of windows over the city lights. There's champagne chillin' within reach, fresh strawberries and some fancy chocolates that just melt in your mouth. Soft stereo music is piped in here and I could've picked from half a dozen different kinds of bubbles—some of them edible, if you can believe that. And you're missin' all this and me, too."

No doubt that she was missing him. She wriggled down a little further in bed, keeping her eyes closed because the vivid image of him in her mind's eye made her feel closer to him. "I saw you ride," she said then. "Are you all right?"

"Cable TV?"

"Satellite—at your place when I picked Danny up to spend the night tonight. Are you okay?"

"Feeling no pain."

"You're drinking?"

He chuckled. "Sorry to ruin my bad-boy reputation, but no, I haven't been drinking. Haven't even touched the champagne. I'm sitting in the warm whirlpool jets of this tub, darlin'. And thinking about some places on your body I'd like to aim 'em."

The thought made her skin tingle. "And you're all by your lonesome . . ." she heard herself say as one bit of flotsam washed ashore.

"Saw Becca, did you?" He laughed.

"And Danny told us how she follows you around."

"She's a piece of work, that one. I don't suppose Danny told you I can't stand the woman."

"Actually, he did." But it sounded better coming from Linc. "He prefers Shelly or Randa."

"Boy has a big mouth," he muttered. "Yes, sweet little Kansas, I am all by my lonesome wishin' for a pointy-chinned woman with a backside that fits just right in the palms of my hands."

"Texas is in short supply?"

"Only one in the whole world, and she'd be here with me right now instead of in rainy Wyoming except that I'm havin' some trouble getting her to let down her hair."

"How'd you know it was raining here?"

"I can hear the thunder in the background."

Kansas had been too immersed in him to notice. She opened her eyes to look out the window and instead found Danny silently standing at the foot of her bed, thumb in his mouth, blanket being rubbed against his nose. "Danny!"

"Let me guess," Linc said from the other end of the line. "You just opened your eyes and found my boy standin' somewhere nearby, staring you down. He does it all the time."

Kansas held the phone's mouthpiece to her chin and said over it, "Did the thunder wake you, sweetheart?"

Danny nodded solemnly.

"Want to sleep in here with me?"

Again the nod just before he climbed up beside her. But on the phone Linc said, "My own son, beatin' my time. Ask him if he'd like to trade me straight across for a penthouse in Texas."

Kansas didn't do any such thing. She said, "Your dad is on the phone. Want to talk to him?"

Once more the sober nod as Danny reached for it.

He was groggy and didn't say much. But being as close as she was, Kansas could hear most of what Linc said to him. Comforting, soothing things, assuring him he was safe and loved, and tugging on Kansas's heartstrings.

Then she heard him say good-night to the little boy and tell him to hand her the phone.

"Bet he's back to sleep already, isn't he?"

She glanced at the pillow beside her. "Curling up and on his way."

"You'll find him snuggled up against you by morning."

Lovely prospect. "That's okay. I don't mind."

"I'm going to expect the same answer for myself when I get back there or you could cause some serious resentment between father and son."

Kansas only laughed.

"I better let you get some sleep and head that way myself. Can't have circles under my eyes for the pictures they're takin' tomorrow—you know the life of a high-ticket model is a demanding one," he said, mocking himself.

"I suppose such a great room has a great bed," she said, not wanting to hang up just yet.

"Huge," he confirmed. "And with some very fancy mirrors in opportune places nearby. Shame they'll be wasted."

But Kansas was relieved to know it.

"Take care of things till I get back, darlin'," he said then.

"That's what I'm good at."

"Oh, you're good at a lot more than that," he said with a lascivious chuckle.

"Night, Linc," she said in a tone that chastised and flirted at once.

"Night, darlin'," he answered.

For the first few minutes after she hung up, Kansas basked in the lingering glow of having talked to him.

But slowly that glow began to fade as the ache of wishing he were there with her inched its way back. And that ache let the tide come in again.

Bringing with it the debris.

For those same few minutes Linc stared at the phone he'd replaced on the hook beside the tub, as if it continued his connection to Kansas.

But the bathwater was getting cold, and he finally opened the drain and got out.

The towel he reached for came from a heated bar and was thicker than most winter coats, and again he marveled at the amenities of the place. It was a far cry from the motel rooms and trailers he was used to when he was rodeoing. This endorsement business had some nice perks.

And yet, perks aside, he wasn't enjoying himself. The place just felt too empty.

That was crazy, he knew. There'd been plenty of times when he'd been alone in a hotel room.

But there was something about this one that was different. Something about this whole trip that was different. And the fact that talking to Kansas just now had both helped while he'd been on the phone, and made it worse now that he wasn't gave him an inkling of what was going on.

Dried off, he went into the bedroom and got into bed. From there he dimmed the lights just enough to leave the room in a hazy golden glow. Lying on his back, his hands behind his head, he stared up at the mirrored ceiling with the gold marbling that made it look more decorative than erotic, and there he was, all alone in that big bed.

Years ago if he'd felt like this—restless and lonely— he'd have gone down to the bar or out to the nearest honky-tonk. He'd have been drinking with the best of them, dancing till dawn, raising hell.

But none of that appealed to him now. It hadn't in a long time. Since Danny'd been born.

And besides, tonight it was Kansas he was craving. Only Kansas that could fill the gap.

He missed Danny, too, of course. As he always did whenever they were separated. But the deep-down longing that was eating at him this trip was for Kansas.

It was as if he'd left behind something vital to his existence.

He felt silly thinking a thing like that. But it was true. Never in his life had he felt so incomplete at not being with someone. There was the damnedest hole in his gut. It was as if the distance between them had set his whole world off kilter.

He closed his eyes and pictured her cuddled up in her bed with Danny, the rain pouring outside the window. Himself with them.

And the rightness of them being a family suddenly struck him like a ton of bricks, as if some force greater than he was showing him what was meant to be.

A part of this emptiness he was feeling, he decided, was the fact that there wasn't any binding tie between himself and Kansas. That he couldn't lie here and count the days until he'd be back in her bed because nothing said he'd ever be there again. He didn't have a claim on her.

But he wanted one.

He wanted to know that each time he left Elk Creek there was no doubt that Kansas would be there waiting for him when he got back. That it was to their own bed he'd be returning. To a home they shared, a home that was more than just a place. A home that was also a woman he loved and who loved and cared for him in return. A woman who asked if he was all right and really meant it. A woman who'd sometimes come along and make a place like this a home, too. A woman with whom he could leave Danny, knowing she loved him as much as if he'd come from her womb.

Kansas.

He really did love her. More than he'd realized before. More than he'd loved Virgie, he admitted sadly. For what he felt for Kansas wasn't merely a sharing of good times without bad, or of only things that were fast and loose and impermanent. What he felt for Kansas was deeper than that. Stronger. The kind of love that would help him weather the storms, the kind of love that he could count on when things got rough the same way he could count on it when life was rosy.

And what he wanted was the bond that would seal it, that would make her his, that would make him and Kansas and Danny a family.

What he wanted, more than he'd ever wanted anything, was for Kansas to be his wife.

Chapter Nine

By Friday the rain stopped and summer reasserted itself in an eighty-five-degree day.

Kansas woke up that morning long before her alarm went off. Her first thought was that within a matter of hours Linc would be home. But her feelings were mixed.

She wished she wasn't excited. Excitement diluted what she'd suffered in the past few days. All the ugly emptiness and loneliness and worry, the awful sense of being only on the sidelines of Linc's life.

And she needed to keep in mind what it had been like, because those were feelings she would have on a regular basis if she went on indulging in this relationship with him.

So instead of letting the excitement get the upper hand, she tamped down on it and thought about Danny's birthday, and all she needed to do for his party that evening. And that was what she tried to keep her thoughts on through the whole day whenever they veered in Linc's direction and her pulse began to race.

She closed the store a little early at the end of that afternoon and went home for a quick change into a pair of cutoff shorts and a sleeveless white blouse.

That was all she meant to do. But somehow on the way past the bathroom she stepped in and took her hair out of the ponytail it was in, brushed it, and let it hang long and free. And while she was there, she decided to try that new lip gloss she'd bought the day before. She might have tried the new blush, too, except that when she looked at her reflection in the mirror she saw that she didn't need any at all.

"But you needed it every other day this week, because you looked as miserable as you felt. That's why you bought it, remember?" she chastised her own image.

Yet even the reminder didn't keep her from driving faster than she should have to the Heller ranch.

Jackson was out front when she drove around the circular driveway, and he headed for the car as she parked. Danny must have been watching for her, because he ran from the open front door a few moments later, exhibiting the same kind of exuberance Kansas was trying not to have.

"Hug," she demanded, hunkering down on her heels so she was at his level.

Danny didn't hesitate. He ran into her arms, squeezing her neck like a vise.

"Happy birthday, sweetheart!" she said with a laugh.

"I'm s'ree now," he informed her, his tone full of accomplishment.

"I know you are. Congratulations."

"An' my dad's comin' home."

"He isn't home yet?" she asked with a sinking feeling, aiming the question at Jackson, who was unloading the rear of the station wagon.

"Expected him, but he's not here," Jackson answered.

Danny let go of Kansas's neck and climbed into the rear of her car to peek into the packing boxes she had loaded with food and party paraphernalia.

"Linc didn't call?" she asked Jackson.

"Haven't heard a word."

"You don't think something might have happened to him, do you?" she whispered so Danny couldn't hear.

"Nah. Probably just got tied up with a flight delay or a luggage claim or something."

Of course that was it, Kansas thought, hating how easily she could be pulled back into the murky emotional waters of the past few days.

Fighting it, she put on a smile as if she weren't really disturbed at all, grabbed the helium balloons and the sack full of presents and went with Jackson and Danny into the house.

By the time Della, Bucky and their kids arrived an hour and a half later, the back patio was decorated with banners of red, blue and yellow, and matching tablecloths, plates, napkins and centerpieces. There were balloons tied to everything, and party favors adorned all of the kids' place settings, along with silly hats, whistles and noisemakers she knew her sister would groan over.

Jackson had told Kansas to call Della and have her bring swimming suits, and so as Kansas and her sister cooked hamburgers on the barbecue grill, Bucky and Jackson put water wings on all the kids and took them for a swim in the pool.

"I haven't been out here in so long I'd forgotten how nice a place it is," Della said on her way to the serving table with a bowl of potato salad.

"It is something, isn't it?" Kansas answered.

"But, uh, aren't we missing someone?"

"Linc was supposed to be back this afternoon." Kansas's own level of uneasiness was rising with each passing hour, and the control she'd been determined to exert over her feelings about him was slipping at the same speed.

Where was he? Why wasn't he here the way he said he'd be? Had something happened? Was he hurt? In trouble?

"Didn't he even call to say he'd be late?" Della asked, breaking into Kansas's thoughts.

"No," Kansas said simply, frowning at the hamburgers she was flipping.

Della didn't say a word to that and Kansas thought her silence carried more weight than anything she could have said.

"He'll be home when he can," she added defensively. "Something unavoidable had to have happened to make him late for Danny's birthday."

Della nodded. "I'm sure. The hazards of travel," she agreed.

But Kansas knew what she was really saying. She was saying that to be involved with a man who made

his living going off to rodeo meant accepting that there
were going to be glitches in getting him home again.
That the least of those glitches was a delayed flight.
She was saying that this was the reality of a life like
Linc led—missing him, pining for him, not having him
there when she needed him to be or when she wanted
him to be. Waiting for him, not knowing where he
might be at any given moment, or whom he might be
with or when he might come home. She was saying
that this was the way things would be—Kansas having to go on without him, acting as if it didn't matter
whether he showed up or not, when it really did matter, a lot, and being disappointed and worried and
anxious and tense—

"Better watch those flames, Kansas," Della advised.

"What? Oh!" Kansas was jolted out of her
thoughts to a raging fire in one section of the barbecue. She spritzed it out with a water bottle.

"I'm sure he's fine and will be here anytime," Della
soothed as if she sensed what had been going through
her sister's thoughts. Then she nodded toward the
pool. "Danny doesn't seem to mind. He's having a
great time."

Kansas looked in that direction, seeing the two men
and the five children in a splashing war—kids against
adults. Danny, in particular, was clearly having fun as
he giggled and slapped water at his uncles. Della was
right: their nephew wasn't disturbed by his father not
being here yet. But that didn't change the fact that
Linc should have been here.

The back door opened just then and Kansas's heart
danced with the certainty that it was Linc.

But when she turned, she found Linc's and Jackson's sister, Beth, coming out. "Anybody home?" she joked as she did.

The fun in the pool stopped while all eyes turned to the new arrival.

"Beth!" Jackson called, hoisting himself out of the water. "It's about time."

Kansas had had that same sentiment on the tip of her tongue, but for a different Heller. She watched as Jackson crossed to his sister and pecked a kiss on her cheek.

"You're just in time for Danny's birthday party."

"Which one is he?" she asked, scanning the small bodies as Bucky herded everyone out to dry off for supper.

"He's the little squirt in the plaid trunks. I'll introduce you when he's dry—when we're all dry."

The swimmers went inside and left Kansas and Della to greet Beth, who gave them both a hug and said how good it was to see them again, pitching in to help put the finishing touches on supper.

Beth was a petite woman, barely two inches over five feet. She had the Heller blue eyes and dark coffee-bean-colored hair. "Where's Linc?" she asked as they took seats at the adults' table.

"Waylaid, I guess," Della answered before Kansas could. "He's due back from a Texas rodeo any minute now. How about your husband? Is he with you?"

Kansas watched her old friend's delicate features tense even though Beth tried for a nonchalant smile. "I'm not married anymore."

"Oh, I hadn't heard. I'm sorry," Della said.

"It's all right. No one knows, actually. Not even Jackson. The divorce was just finalized a short time ago."

The men and kids rejoined them then. Jackson presented Beth to a suddenly shy Danny, who gravitated toward Kansas for moral support before joining his cousins for dinner and leaving this newcomer to the grown-ups.

Kansas was quiet through the meal, her thoughts on Linc and where he might be, her concerns mounting. But Jackson, Bucky and Della had so many questions for Beth that no one seemed to notice.

By the time they were all finished eating, Beth was visibly wilting. Jackson and Bucky took the kids off to explore the helicopter while Kansas and Della cleared the mess and urged Beth to leave them to it and concentrate on getting herself settled in.

After a brief denial, she admitted she needed some rest and said good-night.

The dishes were cleared when the kids came back, ready for the games Kansas had planned. She made sure everyone won something, whether at blindman's buff, or pin the tail on the donkey, or horseshoes, but by dark she'd run out of games and prizes, and the kids were running out of steam.

And still there was no sign of Linc.

"I think we ought to go ahead and let Danny open his gifts and then cut the cake, Kansas," Jackson said then. "I don't know what happened to Linc, but these kids are ready to call it a night."

"I hate to see him miss everything," Kansas answered. But when Bucky and Della added their encouragement and Danny put up a fatigue-induced fit to finally open his presents, she conceded.

Her last hope that Linc would show up was stuffed into the trash can along with the wrappings when Danny finished his paper-tearing frenzy. Linc was not coming, she finally told herself as she went into the kitchen to put the candles on the cake.

"Damn you, you could have at least called," she muttered to herself when she picked up the cowboy-hat-shaped cake and headed for the patio once more.

Jackson turned off the lights for her entrance and everyone began singing "Happy Birthday" as soon as she stepped out the door. Danny's eyes grew round and his tiny face beamed with a delight that was wonderful to see.

But Linc was missing it, Kansas thought. And that fact bled the joy out of her.

Then, halfway through the song, she heard the door at her back open again and a deep bass voice join in with enough vigor to carry the tune alone.

Linc went straight to Danny and hoisted him into his arms for the rest of the song. When it was over, he gave a loud whoop, held Danny over the cake and said, "Happy birthday, son. Blow out your candles," as if he hadn't missed a single moment that had come before.

His arrival breathed new life into the party. For everyone but Kansas. She felt as if her insides had been put through a meat grinder, and on top of all she'd felt through the week, it kept her wary enough to maintain her distance from his charm as never before.

Linc's gifts to Danny were a brand-new, custom-made cowboy hat, boots and a belt buckle that thrilled the little boy to no end because they were like Linc's and Jackson's.

Linc brought all the kids souvenirs from the rodeo and had enough pent-up energy left over to teach them rope tricks until Della and Bucky insisted on taking their brood home.

Kansas was ready to go by then, too, before the sight of Linc's newly sun-bronzed face could change her mind.

"You don't have to go yet, do you?" Linc asked over Danny's head when she joined her sister's good-byes.

"It's been a long day," she answered. "And I'm sure you and Danny want to spend some time alone together before his birthday is over." She hadn't intended to put a rebuke in that last part, but there it was anyway and it made him frown. But what did he expect, she thought, hearts and flowers and open arms to welcome him?

"Kansas?" he said, the simple word infused with a wealth of questions, revealing his confusion.

But she pretended not to notice, blew Danny a kiss good-night, wished him a last happy birthday and left at the same time her sister did.

Kansas was lying in bed, in the dark, trying to sort through all she felt, when she heard knocking on her window almost two hours later.

She nearly jumped out of her skin at the unexpected sound. But she had no doubt that her late-night visitor was Linc even before she opened the curtains and found him sitting on the back porch roof outside.

"How did you get up there?" she asked through the screen as she climbed onto the cushioned window seat and grabbed one of the lacy throw pillows to hug in front of the oversize man's T-shirt she'd worn to bed.

"Would Juliet ask Romeo a question like that? No, she'd just smother him with kisses because she was so glad to see him."

"Not if she was thinking burglars could follow the same path," Kansas countered pragmatically.

Linc nodded over his shoulder. "Trellis. Works as well as a ladder. But when was the last time Elk Creek had a burglary?"

Okay, so he had a point. But being contrary helped her not to pay so much attention to how he looked lounging on her rooftop, one long leg stretched out, the other bent at the knee and bracing his elbow where it burst in muscular glory from his rolled-up chambray shirtsleeve.

He'd changed clothes, she noticed, and now wore clean jeans that were tight all the way down the shank of his boot. A leather vest hung open over his shirt and it was the same color as his newly tanned skin. His hair looked freshly washed and combed, the whisker shadow he'd come home with was gone. He smelled of soap and after-shave, and was altogether the image of a strong, healthy, robust male animal so sexy she could feel her senses kicking into overdrive already. But she fought them mightily.

"Mad at me?" he asked.

She wasn't mad exactly. What was there to be mad about? That he was what he was? That he did what he did? That he'd had some sort of delay in getting home that was no doubt unavoidable? "No, I'm not mad," she answered.

"You're not happy."

No, she wasn't that, either. So what was she? Disappointed, maybe. Disillusioned. But that was her own fault. Linc had never pretended to be anything but what he was. "I'm sorry you missed Danny's birthday," was what she finally settled on—the truth, if only part of it.

"Damn planes and schedules. They canceled my flight because there weren't enough passengers and I either had to wait until tomorrow or do what I did, which was get here by way of North Carolina, Minnesota and Montana, if you can believe it. And I didn't have two minutes between getting off one plane and running to catch another to even call." He looked up at the sky. "And now here I am, finally home, and you're keeping me cooling my heels on your roof."

Cool was right—the day might have been warm but the evening air was a chilly remnant of the rain earlier in the week.

Or was it just finally facing reality that chilled Kansas?

Wondering that kept her from opening the screen.

Instead she said, "Did Danny have a good birthday?"

Linc smiled with only one side of his mouth, as if she were giving him an irresistible challenge. "He wants to have another one tomorrow. Thanks for making it so special for him."

"Is he home sleeping?"

"With his boots on," Linc answered, laughing and making Kansas smile to imagine the picture herself.

"Like his dad's."

"I never sleep with my boots on, darlin', and you know it," he teased.

"I meant the boots are like yours—that's why they're such a big deal to him," she amended, sounding prim again and realizing how unfamiliar that primness was beginning to feel. Strange, she thought, not only did Linc bring out things in her that she didn't know she possessed, but there were old familiar parts of herself that were fading away, too, parts she wasn't sorry to see go no matter how things worked out between her and Linc. She helped the process along by changing her tone to add, "In case you weren't aware of it, your son adores you. It's usually their mothers that they form such an attachment to, but with Danny, the sun rises and sets in you."

"That was my plan," he answered in a suddenly hushed, ragged voice that made Kansas take a closer look at him. What she found were his eyes glistening with moisture just before he let his head fall back and pretended to study the treetops.

"Linc?" she whispered, unsure what to say or do at his unexpected emotion.

He closed his eyes and cleared his throat so the wetness had disappeared when he looked at her again. "I didn't want Danny to feel about me the way I felt about Shag," he said then. "That man never touched me except to deliver punishment. I don't remember a single word of praise from him, and I never had any fun with him. Never. He even growled through Christmases. It was as if when my mother died, what little softness was in him evaporated and he was going to make damn sure every bit of it went out of me and Jackson and even poor Beth, too, when she got past being a baby. Lousy way to raise kids."

"Yes, it is," Kansas agreed quietly.

For a moment neither of them said anything. Linc stared at the treetops again and Kansas stared at him, in glorious profile, his face moon-kissed and wonderful. And she fought the urge to go out on the roof with him, to comfort his old hurts, to confirm how much better a father he was to his son.

Then, as if Linc had used that time to shed the ancient memories on his own, he glanced at her out of the corner of his eye and let his mouth stretch into a leisurely, mischievous grin as he reached into his shirt pocket and brought out something he held hidden in his fist.

"The kids weren't the only ones I bought presents for," he tantalized. "You got one, too. But you can't have it unless you open up that screen and let me in."

The idea danced down her spine and left a trail of glitter. She tried to ignore it. She also tried to remember why she should. "It's late," was all she said, hedging.

He cupped his other hand over the one that held her gift and peeked inside before giving her another of those sidelong looks. "It's awful pretty. Be a shame to miss out on it."

"You really are incorrigible, do you know that?"

"Yes, ma'am," he agreed as if it pleased him. "I'm also tired of sittin' out on this roof where I can't get my arms around you. Or my hands in your hair. Or my lips on yours. Or my body up against you—"

She cut him off. "I've been doing a lot of thinking while you were gone—"

"Well, stop it," he ordered, returning the favor. "I know you, Kansas. You've been going over all the negatives to talk yourself out of us. Now let me in there so I can remind you of the positives." He peeked into his fist once more. "And so I can give you your present."

She knew what would happen if she opened that screen and he came inside. And she knew she shouldn't do it, shouldn't give in to temptation.

But there she was, doing it anyway, not sure why and calling herself every kind of a fool for it at the same time.

"You're bad for me, Linc Heller," she said even as she unlatched the screen and let it swing open.

"Let me see if I can't change your mind because you're so good for me," he answered as he climbed in.

She had to get off the window seat for him to do it. While he did, she went to her closet for her pink-and-white-striped bathrobe, slipping into it before she turned on the lamp on her nightstand. By the time she'd finished all that, he'd relatched the screen and met her at the bedside, his fist held against his chest.

"First we need a proper hello," he said, cupping the back of her head in his free hand as he slowly leaned low enough to press his mouth to hers.

If there was an elixir of life, this was it, Kansas thought, losing herself to the wonder of the kiss that fed her spirit after the past days' fast.

His lips were parted, moist and sweet, drinking as deeply of her as she was of him. She raised her hands to his biceps, big and hard and radiating heat and power. It seemed certain that he'd pull her close then, crush her to him the way he had before, the way she wanted him to.

But he didn't.

He only kissed her. Thoroughly, slowly, magnificently. Awakening desires and yearnings. Quieting doubts. But doing nothing more than kissing her soundly.

When his lips left hers, he smiled an intimate smile and said, "Hello, darlin'. I missed you so much it hurt." Then he let go of her and sat in the armchair in the corner on the other side of the night table.

Kansas had expected that once he got inside, once he got close enough to touch her, to kiss her, they'd end up in bed. She wasn't quite sure what to do when that didn't happen. Sitting even on the edge of the mattress seemed somehow inappropriate, so she returned to the window seat and sat across it, her back against the side wall, her knees drawn up to her chest, feet flat on the cushion.

"I did a fair share of thinking myself while I was gone," he finally said.

She was beginning to wonder if that closed fist of his held anything but air. "What did you do a fair share of thinking about?"

"You. And me. And us. And Danny. And us."

She listened to him talk about not enjoying this trip, about missing her as much as she'd missed him. She listened to him tell her how much he loved her, and the whole time her eyes never left him.

Then he stood and came to the window seat, taking up the other end but angling one leg on the cushion so he faced her.

"Bet you thought when I got in here I was going to take you to bed, didn't you?" he asked with an ornery grin.

Kansas answered with only an arch of her eyebrows.

"Well, I'm not going to do that again until you marry me."

He stretched his arm out, laying the back of his closed fist on top of her upraised knees, and finally opened his hand, where a tiny clear-glass rose lay in his palm. Around its stem, cradled in its leaves, were two matching wedding bands of fine spun gold.

And Kansas was shocked to the core. "Marry you?"

"I love you, Kansas. I want you to be my wife," he said as if all he'd told her before should have made that clear.

Her immediate reaction was to fling herself into his arms, to throw caution to the wind and say yes. She loved him. Loved him more than she'd thought it possible to love anyone.

But she stayed put, except for sitting forward a little to stare at the delicate, perfect rose in the palm of his big, callused hand. "It isn't that easy," she said, fighting hard against the urge to take his gift and hold it to her own heart.

"If you're worried about not being able to have babies, then stop it right now. We have Danny. And if we want more, we'll adopt."

Quick tears sprang to her eyes for that acceptance of her barrenness, for his inclusion of her in the possession of Danny, and it weakened her resistance enough for her to take the rose from his hand. But only tentatively. Only between her thumb and forefinger by the very end of the stem, and only keeping her own arm out straight, away from her.

This time it was Kansas who blinked back the tears and swallowed hard, loving him so much it filled her up, nearly melting her in the heat of his hand turned to cup her knee.

But the days he'd been gone were difficult ones; waiting for him tonight had been miserable, and she'd had a voyeur's view into the other part of his life. Altogether those things had left an indelible doubt.

"How would your rodeoing fit in?" she asked quietly.

The question took him by surprise. It showed in his expression and in the short burst of a laugh. "How would it fit in? Just the way it did this week. I'll go off when I have to and come back when it's over. And I'll keep working on you about going with me now and then."

"I'd have a lifetime of waiting for you, of worrying, of empty days and nights while you're away," she said, adding her viewpoint.

"But you'd know I was coming back."

She'd known that this time, too. It hadn't made the days any fuller or faster. It hadn't helped the loneliness or the worry, or the wondering if another woman might catch him at a vulnerable moment and take her place. "I want a husband who's across the table from me every evening at supper, who's in my bed when I go to sleep at night and there for breakfast the next morning. How many rodeos are there every year, Linc? No, you don't need to answer that—I know there are enough that you'd spend more days away than here, wouldn't you?"

"You can come with me to some of them," he repeated, frowning at her. "And when I'm home we'll have every minute together because I won't be going off to a job."

She shook her head, watching him through full eyes again. "I don't want to be only a part-time wife."

"A part-time wife?" he repeated as if she were out of her mind. "That isn't what I'm askin' you to be."

"Isn't it? I wouldn't be much of a wife to you when you were off on your own and you'd be here only part of the time. What would that make me, if not a part-time wife?"

"I'm in love with you, Kansas," he said vehemently, as if that were the answer to everything. "I want to have a home with you."

"No, you said it right that first night out at the ranch when you were sick—what you want is a home base, not a home. There's a difference."

"Damn it, Kansas, rodeoing is what I do."

"I realize that. I'm not asking you to do anything else. I'm only saying I know myself and what I want well enough to know I'd be unhappy. It goes back to us being different, Linc, to us leading different lives. You want to make me a stopover in yours and I can't be only that."

"You're a hell of a lot more than a stopover to me."

"It wouldn't seem that way."

For a moment his eyes bored into hers and Kansas wondered if she was doing the right thing.

But in the end she took his hand from her knee, turned it palm up and put the ring-wrapped rose back where it had come from.

"It wouldn't be any different if I was a traveling salesman," he pointed out.

"Then neither would my answer."

He closed his fist around the rose in an angry swipe, as if he'd snatched it in midair. "Tell me you don't love me, Kansas," he challenged.

"I wish I didn't," she answered in a voice that cracked.

"And tell me you don't love Danny."

"You know I can't."

"Then, damn it, this doesn't make sense."

"Maybe that's because you wouldn't be the one left behind."

"Think it over," he coaxed in a quieter tone.

"I don't have to. In a way, I've been thinking it over ever since you came back to town, and even more in these past few days. Tonight."

"But we're so good together, darlin'," he seduced, clearly trying a different tack.

"But we wouldn't be together most of the time."

He stood then, his anger and frustration showing. "I want you to be my wife, Kansas," he said in a way that gave an ultimatum.

Her throat clogged and she could barely manage to whisper, "No," before turning her head away from him to hide the tears that blinded her.

But she knew when he left by the hard sound of his boot heels on the floor and the crash of her front door when he slammed out of it.

The sounds made her hug her knees hard against her chest and drop her forehead to the valley between them.

And in the awful silence that remained she couldn't help wondering if she was being a fool.

If having a little of him would have been better than having none at all.

Chapter Ten

Linc nearly slammed the front door to the ranch house, too, when he got home. But at the last minute he caught himself, remembering that he wasn't alone and would wake everybody.

Once he'd closed it—very firmly—he didn't bother to go upstairs, because he knew he couldn't sleep. Instead he fired his keys into one of the couches and stormed through the dining room.

But he stopped short a second time at the door to the kitchen, on the verge of hitting it so fiercely it would have crashed into the wall behind it.

With his hand in midair, he paused, pinched his eyes shut and pointed his chin at the ceiling, while anger, confusion and pain had their way with him.

How could she love him and turn him down anyway?

He took a deep breath to steady himself, dropped his chin, opened his eyes and went through the swinging door soundlessly, flipping on the light switch as he did.

But the kitchen wasn't empty as he'd expected it to be. Beth sat on a stool at the butcher block, her head in her hands until she jolted up like a doe caught in headlights.

"Beth?" Linc said, alarmed at his first sight of her since before Danny was born. She was much too thin, much too pale, and she looked as if she were carrying the weight of the world on her shoulders. But how could that be when he was?

His sister smiled gamely. "Linc," she said, forcing brightness. "I didn't hear you come in."

He wasn't completely in yet—he was still in the doorway. But he stepped through it then, going to kiss her cheek. "We've been wondering when you'd get here."

"I had a lot to do before I could leave."

"Mmm," he muttered knowingly. He patted her arm before crossing to the cupboard for a glass. "I saw your car outside when I got home earlier. Looks like everything you own is in it."

"It is."

"Problems at home?"

A wry laugh escaped and she glanced around the room. "This is home again. Ash and I split up."

That got a rise out of his eyebrows. "Did I miss something?"

"Are you kidding? You miss everything, traveling around the way you do," she teased. "But this time no one knew. I haven't even told Jackson, and I skirted everybody else's questions tonight, too, so I wouldn't put a damper on the party. But it's the way things are, just the same.''

Linc poured himself ice tea, took a jar of pickled beets out and brought both to the butcher block. He swung one leg over a stool across from Beth's and opened the jar, offering her one in spite of the fact that she had a glass of milk in front of her—it didn't look as if she'd touched it.

But she recoiled and shook her head.

''You used to love these things,'' he said.

''Not tonight,'' she answered as if fighting the rise of her gorge.

''And I've never seen you drink milk in your life. Not even when we were kids.''

She looked at the glass as if it were poison, wrinkling her nose at it. ''You aren't seeing that tonight, either.''

Linc set the jar in front of him, but it occurred to him that the gnawing in the pit of his stomach wasn't really hunger at all and he took only a drink of tea. ''Are we talking separation or divorce?''

''Divorce. Signed, sealed and done with.''

''What hap—''

''The details don't matter,'' she cut him off. ''The marriage didn't work out and now it's over.''

''And you're moving back to Elk Creek, too?''

''*Too?* Who else is?''

''Danny and me.''

That made her laugh genuinely. ''Poor Jackson. How do you think he's going to feel about all of us moving in on him for good?''

''I'm not.''

''You aren't living here?''

''I am for now, but not for good.''

Beth smiled. "Things are that serious between you and Kansas?"

Linc felt a storm cloud gather around his heart all over again. "Seriously in trouble," he muttered darkly, more to himself than to his sister. "I asked her to marry me tonight. But she turned me down."

"Oh, Linc, I'm sorry."

"Yeah. Me, too. Damn it." He ran his hands through his hair, pulling it back so tight it almost hurt. But that kind of pain was better than the emotional kind. Then he let go of his head and his temper. "I just don't understand it!" he railed suddenly. "I love her. She loves me. She loves Danny. Danny's crazy about her—"

"So what's the problem?"

"She says she doesn't want to be a part-time wife."

"Mmm." This time it was Beth who nodded knowingly. "Your rodeoing and traveling all the time. I suppose you were proposing that she keep the home fires burning and raise Danny while you're off following the circuit."

He narrowed his eyes at his sister, not appreciating the sound of that. "I'm not looking to pawn off my son on anyone."

"I didn't say you were. But if Danny is home with Kansas and you're gone most of the time, she's the one who'll be doing the raising, isn't she?"

He hadn't looked at it that way. And he definitely didn't like the perspective. He didn't answer her, instead he just stared into his glass.

"How about you?" Beth asked then.

"How about me what?"

Beth shrugged. "I was looking out my bedroom window when they sang happy birthday to Danny. I saw you come in and pick him up. I saw you playing with him. I saw him hanging on to you. The two of you are close, aren't you?"

Linc frowned at her. "It isn't anything like you and Jackson and I were with Shag, that's for sure."

"I also saw you watching Kansas, following her every move with your eyes. And I know the minute you got Danny to sleep you rushed through a shower and shave and ran out of here as if your tail was on fire. You couldn't wait to get to her."

"Did you take up spying on that Indian reservation?"

"Didn't have to. It was all right out there for anyone to see."

"What's your point?"

"I'm just wondering, in view of how much you seem to care for them both and enjoy them, how you feel about being a part-time husband and father."

He stared at her, letting what she'd said sink in.

A part-time husband and father.

Even when Kansas had referred to herself that way, it hadn't occurred to him that it would apply to him, too. It rocked him slightly to realize it and he went from frowning at his sister to frowning into his ice tea glass again.

Beth gave a self-mocking chuckle that was really only a burst of air. "I'm the last person to think I can give advice, Linc. But I can tell you one thing. Whatever imperfections exist going into a marriage, marriage only makes them worse. Better to hammer through them before and find a solution, if there is one."

"And if there isn't one?" he asked from deep inside the pit of despair.

"Then maybe getting married isn't a good idea. Because divorce is no fun at all."

Linc watched without comment as his sister took her milk to the sink and poured it down the drain. Then she headed for the door to the dining room. "I'm going to try to sleep. Again. Maybe you should, too. Things might look different to you in the morning."

He nodded but he didn't believe either that he could sleep or that a new day would make him feel any better. "Right behind you," he said anyway, picking up his own glass and the jar of beets.

"Good night," Beth called on her way out.

"Night," he answered over his shoulder as he put the beets back in the fridge.

He did go upstairs, though, straight to Danny's room, where he slipped silently in to check on his son in the dim glow of a night-light.

The little boy slept soundly, his mouth slightly open, his thumb nearby, as was his raggedy old blanket. The covers were all at the bottom of the bed, and along with his pajamas, he still wore his cowboy boots.

The sight made Linc smile as nothing else could at that moment, and his heart swelled with love for his son.

Carefully he slipped off the boots and pulled the sheet and blanket up to the tiny shoulders, tucking Danny in.

As he did, Linc thought that he'd missed tucking him in the nights he'd been away. But then he'd missed Danny and everything about him. The trip to Texas was the longest they'd ever been apart.

He hunkered down on his heels and watched the little boy sleep, one arm on the pillow above Danny's head, touching him only with his own thumb running slowly back and forth across the tiny brow.

A part-time father. A part-time husband.

He'd come back to Elk Creek because he knew Danny needed roots, stability, a place to grow up where the faces didn't change, the surroundings stayed the same, where he had a sense of belonging to more than Linc and the next hotel room. A home base.

That's all he'd thought about—giving Danny that kind of foundation.

But now he had to face it.

Kansas was right. Beth was right.

How many nights would go by that he wouldn't be there to tuck Danny in? How many of his son's birthdays would he be late for or miss entirely? Danny had regaled him with the party doings, with a story about a splashing war with Jackson and Bucky, with helping Jackson around the ranch, with baking cookies with Kansas.

How much more of that would he miss? Linc asked himself. How much of his son's childhood?

Danny seemed to have fared pretty well without him. That part of his thinking had proved right—it was easier for the boy to be left rooted in a place where he had other family to love and care for him while Linc was away, to fill the gap.

But Linc hadn't done nearly as well.

He'd missed Danny. Missed his company, having him with him to check out the stock, to watch the other events, to share meals, having him there when it was time to go back to the hotel room. And not only that, but he hadn't liked coming home to find how easily he'd been displaced in his son's life, either.

He knew it was irrational to resent the very thing he'd wanted to happen, but he did. He felt as if he'd been left out, as if he were dispensable. And he didn't like it. Didn't like that Danny had enjoyed so much with other people. Without his father.

And what about Kansas? What about being a part-time husband to her?

He'd missed her every bit as much as Danny. So much it had been an ache in his bones. Hell, he'd only slept with her once, and yet every night in Texas he'd gone to sleep hugging a pillow and imagining it was her.

Did he want fewer of the nights in her bed than of those out of it? He didn't, that was for damn sure. Any more than he wanted not to be around to buy her box suppers or to dance with her or to sit with her on her porch on balmy summer nights.

He didn't want to miss anything with her, either. Or to know that when he wasn't there for her, someone else just might be.

So, no, he guessed being a part-time father or a part-time husband wasn't appealing to him.

But what was the alternative?

He bounced up to his feet to leave Danny's room and that question he couldn't face.

Of course Danny stayed put, but the question went with him just the same.

He didn't bother to turn on the light in his own bedroom. His drapes were open and moonlight spilled in through the window, directly onto his gear where he'd just dropped it on the floor when he'd gotten home tonight.

His saddle was slung over the top of his suitcase and the time-softened, stained leather seemed to be waiting for him like an old friend.

He crossed to it and again hunkered down on his heels, the same way he had at his son's bedside, caressing the curve of the seat.

Lordy, but he loved rodeoing. Everything about it. The sights, the smells, the noise, the excitement, the risk, the rush. And he was good at it. The best around these days.

How could he walk away from that? And to what?

To Kansas. To Danny, a little voice in the back of his mind answered.

But what went unanswered was if he could really walk away.

And in all ornery Shag had taught him, in all the lessons he'd learned himself—most of them the hard way—he didn't know how to choose between doing what he'd dearly loved all his adult life, and being with the woman and child he couldn't love more if he tried.

Kansas hadn't slept a wink all night. When she heard the morning paper hit the front porch just before dawn, she decided it was too late to keep trying and got up.

She took a long bath, hoping the warm water would make her feel better. But it could only help the outside of her. Inside she was still a raw open wound.

"You knew from the start that it wasn't wise to get involved with Linc," she told herself as she stepped out of the tub.

Then she caught sight of her reflection in the mirror and her gaze dropped automatically to that hated scar, studying it as she hadn't since the night Linc had made love to her.

She remembered how much easier he'd made it to accept, and she couldn't be sorry for the time she'd spent with him, for making love with him, for loving him.

And as she had again and again throughout the night, she doubted her decision.

She closed her eyes and laid her forehead against the cool glass of the mirror, hugging her naked body. She forced herself to remember all the reasons she'd turned him down, knowing she'd been right to do it, no matter how it hurt.

But she wasn't going to cry. Not any more. Her eyes couldn't take it and her cheeks were getting chapped.

She took a deep breath, sighed it out and stood up straight. Maybe she'd open the store early, clean out the back room, wash the windows, change the displays—

That was the best thing to do—keep too busy to think, to feel. And leave herself so exhausted by tonight that she'd have to sleep.

She braided her hair, used the new blush to camouflage the pallor in her cheeks and then dressed in a pair of jeans and a striped shirt.

On the way downstairs she considered breakfast but knew she couldn't eat anything. A cup of tea was about as much as her knotted stomach would be able to handle. Tea and a glance at the morning news to keep her mind off Linc, and then she'd go to work.

When she reached the entrance, she opened the front door to get the paper and stopped short. "Linc?"

He was sitting slumped low in one of the wicker chairs, his legs stretched out and crossed at the ankles. His arms were locked over his stomach and his hat covered his face.

The only thing that moved when she said his name was one arm as he lifted a single thumb to his hat brim and pushed the Stetson until it rested back on his head instead. Then he met Kansas's eyes with his own weary-looking ones. "Your paperboy has a great left-handed pitch."

"You haven't been out here all night?"

"Only half of it. Make me a cup of coffee and I'll tell you about it."

It struck her suddenly that rejecting his proposal didn't mean she was never going to see or talk to him again, not in a place the size of Elk Creek. And that wasn't going to be easy, feeling the way she did about him. She didn't think she could be just friendly or neighborly. But if she couldn't marry him or be friendly or neighborly, what did that leave? A small-town feud? A cold war? She didn't want that, either. "Oh, Linc, what are we going to do?" she blurted out suddenly, not meaning to give voice to her lament.

He hoisted himself from the chair, went to the edge of the porch, swept off his hat and sailed it with perfect aim into the back of his pickup truck where it was parked in her driveway. Then he came to her, running his hands through his hair and smiling lovingly from a handsome, exhausted face she had to fight not to raise a caressing palm to.

"You're going to make me a cup of coffee and I'm going to tell you you were right and what I've come up with in the past five hours of soul-searching."

She couldn't imagine a solution. But then, she couldn't imagine living in Elk Creek with him and pretending she didn't love him, didn't want him with all her heart, no matter what she'd said the night before. So she merely held the door open to him and then led the way to her kitchen.

While she made his coffee, she listened to him talk about his late-night conversation with his sister, about realizing he didn't want to be a part-time husband or father any more than she could settle for being a part-time wife.

He'd just said that when she handed him his coffee and for a moment he didn't say any more. He stood leaning against the counter, holding the mug like a water glass and staring at some spot in the distance.

Kansas fixed her tea and took it with her to the kitchen table, sitting down and inviting him to do the same.

He accepted the invitation, bringing his mug but setting it on the table so he could lean forward in the chair, his legs spread, forearms to knees, hands clasped in between. "Will you marry me if I give up rodeoing and stay put?"

Her spirits took an initial leap of joy.

But then they landed on rock-solid earth.

"You love rodeoing. You told me so yourself and I saw it when I watched you on television. Giving it up would be like cutting off your arm."

"Not having you would be like cutting out my heart."

Those quicksilver tears sprang to her eyes with the depth of emotion in his voice, and it would have been easy for Kansas to just accept his sacrifice. If only she hadn't seen his face after that ride.

"You'd be miserable," she said when she'd blinked away the moisture. "You're talking about giving up what we both know you don't want to give up, to live a porch-sitting life that you're not suited to. It might be all right for a little while, Linc. You might even enjoy it the way you have since you got back, but it wouldn't last. Not forever."

"I thought of that, too," he admitted. "And you're right. I truly relish a little porch sitting, but that would change if it was all I ever did. So I asked myself what I'd do if I didn't rodeo. Ranch with Jackson? Nah, couldn't stand that every day. I had a craw full of it as a boy with Shag. Could I help you run the store? Me, a shopkeeper? It doesn't fit. There's the mill, but it's running just fine without me. We need help with the business end of all Shag left, but that's Beth's department—accounting and record keeping and investments. Put me in a boardroom and I'd suffocate."

He looked down at his hands, shaking his head. "I was beginning to feel pretty useless. Started to wonder what I'm good at besides hanging onto the back of a buckin' bronc for eight seconds."

Kansas's heart went out to him and she felt guilty for her part in his self-doubt. But before she could think what to say, he went on.

"Then I remembered dancin' with you in that old holding barn and talking about turning it into a honky-tonk."

"A honky-tonk," she repeated cautiously.

"Put that chin back, Kansas."

"A honky-tonk," she said yet again, as if trying on something that didn't fit.

"Do you love me, Kansas? Do you want to marry me?"

"Yes, I love you and want to marry you. But a honky-tonk—the city council will ask if a loud, late-night liquor-selling establishment is really what Elk Creek needs. Or wants. Or what's best for it."

"The city council will ask that or you will?"

All right, she'd tried to couch it in less personal terms, but it was true—the idea wasn't a plum she was any more anxious to pick than half of town would be. "And what about Danny? Is a place like that good for him to be raised around?"

"It'd keep me here for him—a full-time father instead of a part-time one." He looked up at her from beneath his brows. "And it'd keep me a full-time husband," he added pointedly.

"But would it keep you happy?"

"Happier than being away from you and Danny."

"Oh, Linc, I want to believe that." But she was afraid to. Afraid of what would be down the road. "I want to believe it will always be that way. But you've loved rodeoing your whole life. When the newness of being back here, of me, of a honky-tonk, wears off, what if you're sorry? What if you miss it, if you resent not doing it anymore?"

"I'll keep a hand in it. I'll go a time or two a year when the itch gets bad."

So he expected to pine for it. That didn't help reassure her. "But a rodeo rider is what you are. You're not a saloon owner."

"And neither are you. Is that what you're saying, Kansas?"

Yes, that was part of what she was saying. But she didn't want to admit it, because he seemed to think that was more important than her concerns for him and what he was thinking of giving up, and it wasn't.

He pinned her with eyes that bored into her. "I'm in love with you, and I want you to be my wife. I love Danny more than anyone could have told me was possible before I had him. I don't want to be away from either of you, and so I had to pick between that and rodeoing. Yes, I love rodeoing. But not more than I love the two of you."

He stood suddenly, clasping her arms to take her with him, squeezing so tight it seemed as if he thought that might urge her to do what he wanted. "The holding barn is far enough on the outskirts of town not to disturb anybody, and we can do it so it isn't seedy or a bad influence on Danny or anyone else. We can make it a place to go to hear some good music and dance—there's nothing wrong with that."

"We? Are you wanting me to give up the store, too?" she asked in alarm.

"No, and don't look so worried. I'm not going to have you waiting tables or washing dishes or bartending—unless you want to."

"No, I wouldn't."

Something about the way she said that made him smile. "You can just be my watchdog to keep the place respectable. How would that be?"

Her expression must have shown her continuing doubts, because he searched her eyes with his but didn't wait for an answer before going on. "I know being the wife of a honky-tonk owner isn't how you saw yourself. A teacher's wife. A minister's wife, maybe. But this is middle ground for us, darlin'. Sure, it'll make your life a little livelier than you planned, and the hours won't be nine to five, but it'll keep me in Elk Creek and in your bed every night—even if it will be late before I get there. But I'll do everything I

can to have us live a normal life if you'll just come out
of that damn shell of yours and do it. Do it for us
both.''

''I don't know—''

''I'm staying, Kansas. Whether you marry me or
not. I'm giving up rodeoing to make a home for
Danny. Be a part of that.''

What she was a part of was a traditional, quiet,
workaday, churchgoing existence, and he was right—
to accept this was a big change for her. But it was an
even bigger change for him. She had to give up her vision of her future, stretch the boundaries of her values. He had to give up his whole way of life. And that
worried her very, very much. What if this middle
ground was the wrong place for them both to be?

''Tell me you'll think about it,'' he said when confusion and indecision kept her silent. ''Tell me you're
taking back your no to my proposal and will consider
it?''

Kansas looked up into the face she loved. The face
of temptation and all the fear that brought with it.
He'd already put a crack in the shell he wanted to lure
her out of. But what if she actually let him?

''Tell me, darlin','' he beckoned.

''Yes, I'll think about it,'' she finally said, knowing she'd dared to step to the edge of the fissure with
those words.

He smiled, a slow, weary thing. ''I love you,'' he
said forcefully, as if to brand it on her brain. ''Don't
think about a single thing without remembering that.
And how good we are together.''

He kissed her to prove it and the sparks that glittered all through her at the feel of his mouth over hers,
at his hands on her, at the very nearness of his body,

left no question of the power of what was between them.

On its own, her palm rose to the side of his face the way she'd wanted to touch him when she'd first set eyes on him on her porch. Lord, but it couldn't be good to love someone so much!

His lips left hers, came back and left again. "Take a chance on us, darlin'," he whispered, covering her hand with his to lower it from his face.

He kissed her palm and set the glass rose in that very spot, closing her fingers around it and kissing her knuckles as if to seal the promise he'd just laid in her hand.

His wonderful mouth stretched into a smile, and his eyes bathed her in love for only a moment before he turned and left her to the sound of his departing footsteps again, though this time her front door was closed quietly.

Kansas looked down at her closed fist, opening it very slowly.

There, just where he'd put it, was that rose. Beautiful. Delicate. Twined with the rings that could make Linc hers forever.

If only she could believe it wouldn't be a mistake.

Chapter Eleven

"Oh, Kansas, a roadhouse?" Della said with a grimace when Kansas told her about Linc's proposals—for marriage, for giving up rodeoing and for his own future in Elk Creek.

Kansas had called her sister and asked her to come because she needed a sounding board, but now she wondered if Della had been the right choice. Or was it just that she'd wanted someone to talk her out of the doubts that had grown stronger with each hour since Linc had left her that morning and Della was only confirming them?

"You wouldn't even accept the liquor license the town *offered* you," Della reminded her over the lunch she'd brought into the store for them. "Not even just to sell beer. Not even when it would have increased your profits at least a quarter all on its own."

That was true. Instead Sonny Parker had taken the license and turned the empty space next to his barber shop into a liquor store. Now he was driving a brand-new, expensive car. Not that Kansas cared. She'd never once regretted her decision. Liquor had not been what she wanted to contribute to her community.

"And there's all the people it'll bring into town, and the brawls that happen in a place like that. And what about any kind of family life? You'd work days and get home just when he was leaving. He'd be gone till the early hours of the morning and then sleep all day. To see him you'd have to hang out in his bar. And there's Danny..."

Kansas listened to her sister go on with a litany of negatives that matched her own list. But somehow it sounded so...well, so priggish coming from someone else.

She found herself refuting it all with Linc's arguments, in spite of the fact that she still wasn't sure she agreed with them.

"Okay, so you're sure that between the two of you you could make it a respectable place," Della said to curb her defense.

"Well, not *sure*, exactly—"

"Put aside the honky-tonk and let's just talk about his giving up rodeoing and settling down. How long do you think it's going to be before he misses it too much and leaves anyway?"

For that Kansas didn't have an argument.

"I know I said I wasn't going to say another word against him, but he's impulsive, Kansas. That's part of his charm. But the same impulsiveness that made him decide to chuck it all and stay here is likely to cause him to chuck you and the notion of settling down, and take off again." Della finally stopped talking and seemed to wait for Kansas's input. When it didn't come, she said, "Say something. You look like I've lost you."

What could she say? "It worries me," she admitted.

"It should do more than worry you. It should stop you cold. The two of you are as different as—"

"Pickles and peanut butter," Kansas filled in what she'd thought herself from early in her attraction to Linc.

"You live in two different worlds," Della went on. "And you're trying to force them to mesh. But it won't work. Believe me, I wish it would. I've seen the change being with Linc has made in you, how much better you feel about yourself, and I'm grateful to him for that. But what happens when his rodeo fever strikes and he can't resist it—and you know it will eventually. What happens to you then?"

"He says when the urge gets too bad, he'll go to one or two, and Danny and I will just go along, like a vacation."

"And then he'll want to go to one or two more, and then more after that, and before long you'll have the same choices Virgie had—either travel with him constantly or stay alone waiting."

Lord, but it was hard to hear her own fears spoken from her sister's mouth.

"Take the positive things he brought with him this time and keep them," Della urged. "Go on feeling like a desirable, attractive woman again, because that's what you are. But don't get in any deeper and let him hurt you later."

"But what if he really does settle down and stay the way he says he is?" Kansas reasoned. "What if he and Danny are here forever for me to see every day, but only from a distance? What if Linc takes up with someone else, because you know a man like that isn't going to be alone for long? What if I have to spend the rest of my life watching someone else have the family that could have been mine?"

Della cut her off. "Don't use fear tactics to talk yourself into this. Look at the facts, Kansas. Look at how he's spent his life up till now. Look at the way he's hedging by saying he'll go to a rodeo or two still. And don't get dreamy eyed over Danny and being a family," she added. "Remember that boy is still Linc's. And no matter what he says now, when he goes, he'll take Danny with him, and you'll suffer a double loss."

Sort of like the double blow there was in hearing that.

Della must have realized how harsh her words had been, because her eyes teared up with what looked like regret, and she reached across to cover Kansas's hand with her own. "I'm sorry to say these things, honey. I wish none of it were true. But I can see how much you care for that man and that little boy and all you have pinned on them. And it scares me. It scares me that you're going to wrap your arms around smoke."

"And fall flat on my face," Kansas added with a forced laugh to lighten the tone.

Della didn't answer that, but the forlorn and worried expression on her face made it obvious just how disastrous she was convinced marrying Linc would be.

Kansas didn't know what else to say, either. A part of her agreed with Della.

But a part of her didn't.

And then Della's four kids came bounding into the store with Bucky, and Kansas was spared having to say any more at all.

* * *

What remained of the afternoon dragged by for Kansas in spite of how busy she kept herself. Too busy to think, just the way she'd planned before finding Linc on her porch with the morning newspaper.

She closed the store at six and went home, tired to the bone and by then wishing Linc Heller had never come back to Elk Creek to tempt her and cause her such miserable confusion.

As she climbed the steps to her front porch, she heard her name called from the street. She turned just as the Franklin family from two doors down rode by on their bicycles—Sherman, Jodie and their six-year-old, Sally.

Kansas waved and said hello, watching as they continued in the direction of the town square, a picnic basket strapped to the back of Sherman's bike.

That was the life she wanted. Right there. And her gaze hung on to it until they rode out of sight, while her mind's eye pictured herself and Linc and Danny in the Franklins' place.

But would it really be that way? Wouldn't Linc be headed off to work now instead? To a honky-tonk that half the town would disapprove of?

Or even if she and Linc and Danny could spend a few early evening hours together before Linc left, how many of those times would they have before he was bored with such mundane fare and left Elk Creek altogether for the excitement of a rodeo?

Kansas went into the house with the weight of her doubts on her shoulders. They seemed to make her steps heavier, and the hollow echo of them on the hardwood floor made the place seem all the emptier.

What had Linc said about making her life a little livelier?

At that moment it was a very appealing prospect, no matter what the eventuality.

She kicked off her shoes and fell onto the sofa like a rag doll, resting her head against the back and closing her eyes.

"What am I going to do?" she moaned.

She knew what she wanted to do. She wanted to marry Linc, to mother Danny.

Just how great was the risk that it would end badly, that Linc would be unhappy and take off on the rodeo circuit after all?

In asking herself that, she had a sudden picture of a younger Linc Heller. Wildcat Heller. Hell-raiser Heller. The Linc Heller he had been in the past.

But that wasn't who he was now.

Linc had changed, she realized.

She'd spent so much time noticing the things about him that had stayed the same—the potent charm, his love of life and a good time, his energy, his high spirits—that she'd overlooked what wasn't the same.

All of those things were packaged in a grown man now, an adult. A person who proved his maturity and responsibility in the way he parented his son.

And what about Danny?

He was a stronger factor than she'd been giving credit to, she thought now. Would Linc really go back to following the rodeo circuit and take Danny with him when he'd come back to Elk Creek so Danny could have a home, a stable, rooted life, and an opportunity to get to know his extended family? Did she really believe that Linc would go back on that for any kind of selfish reasons?

No, she knew without a doubt that Linc would always do what was best for Danny. And what was best for Danny was just what Linc had proposed to her.

But even if she believed Linc would stay the way he said he would, could she believe that he'd be happy? Could she believe that she was capable of helping him be happy?

The answer to that was a little frightening to her, because she knew she could, but it would take coming out of that shell he'd accused her of being in. It would take her help and approval and support of his honky-tonk. It would take her acceptance and indulgence in those times he needed to do some rodeoing.

It would take some change on her part.

Kansas opened her eyes as if to face the sudden fear of that.

Could she leave behind the old-fashioned, quiet, subdued, conventional person she'd always been and emerge a woman who led a more unconventional existence married to a good-time honky-tonk owner? Could she be that open and liberal? That adaptable? That daring?

But hadn't she already discovered new capacities for those things in herself?

She had, surprising herself. And even more, she'd also already left behind other aspects of her old persona, things she'd been glad to shed—some of the primness, some of the inhibitions...

"So I really have changed, too," she said out loud, confirming what she'd thought only fleetingly when it had occurred to her before.

A shiver went up her spine, but it wasn't caused by dread. It was delicious awakening. That same thing she felt when she was with Linc, when he was dancing with her in a dusty old holding barn or when he was bidding outrageously on her box supper, or climbing in her bedroom window, or just resting those sparkling blue eyes on her in that way he had.

He brought out the best in her.

And she realized that if she didn't marry him, she'd be giving up more than the man she loved, more than the child she loved, more than what she really wanted. She'd be giving up those new parts of herself and slipping back into the shell that had molded her up until Linc Heller had cracked it.

And she didn't want that any more than she wanted to lose Linc.

She shot off the couch with a sudden surge of energy and went into the kitchen, where the glass rose was a tiny centerpiece in the middle of the table. She picked it up and held it in front of her.

"A honky-tonk," she said speculatively. "Well, I guess if a liquor store didn't corrupt Elk Creek, that won't, either."

Then she closed her fist around the ring-wrapped rose and brought it to her heart while she returned to the living room in search of her shoes.

It was Jackson who answered the door at the Heller ranch when Kansas got there. Tall and stoic, he said only her name in greeting, and that as somberly as if they were at a funeral. It caused the oddest urge in Kansas to laugh. Maybe she and the eldest Heller son weren't so much alike. At least not anymore.

"You know, Jackson, I think you might need someone to liven up your life," she said as she controlled the impulse to giggle so as not to insult him.

Jackson stepped aside to let her in. "Linc's out back," he answered in the same even tone of voice, as if she'd asked him where his brother was, and this time Kansas couldn't suppress the laughter bubbling inside her.

"Thanks," she said.

She made a beeline through the house to the door that opened onto the patio. But there she stopped.

She had a perfect view of the pool, where Linc was teaching Danny to swim in the shallow end, and for a moment, she savored the sight.

Danny wore the water wings he'd used at his birthday party while Linc had him kicking and practicing the breast stroke as if he were keeping himself afloat. Linc's deep voice came to her as he coached and praised and teased by turns, and she couldn't help smiling as her heart swelled.

They'll be mine, she thought, taking in the picture of the little boy and the big man, who stood with his broad, bare chest above the water, his hair only damp, the chiseled planes of his face relaxed and happy.

Very happy, she noted. Every bit as happy as his expression had been after that winning ride at the Texas rodeo. In that instant she knew she'd been silly to think that rodeoing—no matter how important to him—was more important than Danny.

And it occurred to her at the same moment that she held an equal place in his heart. That she was just as important to him, and the knowledge of that was a gift greater than anything she could ever have received.

Still she stood there watching them, wondering how she could ever have considered not having the two of them in her life as fully as Linc had offered.

She finally went out to the poolside. But once she got there, the desire to be a part of their fun overcame her and she kept on going, down the corner steps into the brink.

"Kansas!" Danny shouted as he and his father watched in surprise. "You don't gots on a swimmin' suit! Dad! Kansas is gittin' in wis her clothes!"

Linc's grin was like a beacon drawing her to him and on she went until she stood directly in front of him.

"Have you gone a little crazy, darlin'?" he asked as if he heartily approved.

"Maybe just a little," she answered.

"Crazy in love? Crazy enough to marry me?"

"Maybe. Maybe even crazy enough to help you open your honky-tonk."

It hadn't seemed possible for his grin to get any bigger, but it did. "Kansas is going to marry us, Danny," he said to his son without glancing away from her, and without touching her, either, she noted. "What do you say to going to a wedding?"

"Can I wear my new boots and hat?" the little boy asked as stoically as his uncle.

"A born romantic," Linc said in an aside. Then again to Danny, "I don't know. We'll have to see about that."

Still his gaze stayed on her, as if he were savoring the sight along with the moment and was afraid to move and disturb it. "What'll people say when they find out their storekeeper did a thing like this?" he asked then.

"What? Got in a pool with her clothes on or accepted your proposal?"

"Both."

"They'll say just what you did, that I'm out of my mind."

"Will you care?"

"There are other things I care more about."

"And then there's Della. She won't like being my sister-in-law again."

"She'll get used to it."

He laughed as if he'd been testing her and she'd passed. And then, finally, he wrapped his arms around her and closed the gap between them. "Well, you never fail to surprise me, Kansas Daye."

That sobered her some. "I hope I never do."

Only his eyebrows frowned down at her. "Are you worryin' about somethin'?"

"That you might get bored."

He laughed once more. "Well, if I do, I don't think it'll be too much trouble to come up with a way to fix it," he answered, his tone low and sensual and suggestive.

He kissed her then, his lips cool and soft. But it was a brief kiss before he raised up to look her in the eye again, his expression serious.

"I'm in love with you, Kansas. Tell me for the record—will you marry me?"

"For the record?" she repeated as if that put some glitch in it.

He squeezed her to prompt the answer he wanted.

"Okay, for the record—yes, Linc Heller, I will marry you." She pulled away from him enough to take the glass rose from her shirt pocket much the way he had on both the occasions he'd given it to her. "But don't squeeze me again or I could be mortally wounded."

He took the rose and pressed it to his lips for only a moment before tucking it back into her pocket, sending sudden sparks all through her with that simple contact with her breast.

Then he cupped the back of her head in his hands and brought her up to meet him as he bent to capture her mouth again.

This time he lingered, parting his lips over hers in a long, slow kiss that was so sweet it made her ache inside.

She slid her palms up his chest, reveling in the feel of him, and the rest of the world seemed to recede as she lost herself in his touch, his nearness, the bliss of his mouth. How could she ever have survived without this? Without him? she wondered. Because no matter what her foolish mind had thought, there was nothing as wonderful or as worth any risk as to be forever in his arms.

Then they were interrupted when Danny paddled his way into their watery embrace. "Le's play splash or sumthin'," he said as if this game of theirs was no fun at all.

With an arm still around Kansas, Linc picked up his son and then pulled her back close enough for Danny to hook an elbow around each of their necks.

"Behave yourself and welcome Kansas to our family," he told his son.

Danny put his nose nearly to the tip of hers, looked her very solemnly in the eye and said, "I dunno was tha' means," making them both laugh.

And in that moment, when Kansas had one of her own arms around Linc and one around Danny, the emptiness that had been inside of her for so long seemed to disappear, taking with it any lingering fears of the future with Linc.

For in her heart she knew that whether Danny understood or not, the three of them, together as a family, was the way they were meant to be.

* * * * *

Linc and Kansas tie the knot—and Beth Heller finds love—in Book Two of A RANCHING FAMILY. Watch for Baby, My Baby, *available in March 1995, only from Silhouette Special Edition!*

COMING NEXT MONTH

#925 FOR THE BABY'S SAKE—Christine Rimmer
That Special Woman!
Andrea McCreary had decided to raise her unborn baby on her own. Clay Barrett had generously offered a proposal of marriage, and soon realized their arrangement would not be without passion....

#926 C IS FOR COWBOY—Lisa Jackson
Love Letters
Only the promise of a reward convinced Sloan Redhawk to rescue headstrong, spoiled Casey McKee. He despised women like her—yet once he rescued her, he was unable to let her go!

#927 ONE STEP AWAY—Sherryl Woods
Only one thing was missing from Ken Hutchinson's life: the woman of his dreams. Now he'd found Beth Callahan, but convincing her to join his ready-made family wouldn't be so easy....

#928 ONLY ST. NICK KNEW—Nikki Benjamin
Alison Kent was eager to escape the holiday hustle and bustle. Meeting Frank Bradford—and his adorable twin sons—suddenly showed her this could indeed be the most wonderful time of the year!

#929 JAKE RYKER'S BACK IN TOWN—Jennifer Mikels
Hellion Jake Ryker had stormed out of town, leaving behind a broken heart. Stunned to discover he had returned, Leigh McCall struggled with stormy memories—and with Jake's renewed passionate presence.

#930 ABIGAIL AND MISTLETOE—Karen Rose Smith
Abigail Fox's generous nature never allowed her to think of herself. Her heart needed the kind of mending only Brady Crawford could provide—and their kiss under the mistletoe was just the beginning....

MILLION DOLLAR SWEEPSTAKES (III)

No purchase necessary. To enter, follow the directions published. Method of entry may vary. For eligibility, entries must be received no later than March 31, 1996. No liability is assumed for printing errors, lost, late or misdirected entries. Odds of winning are determined by the number of eligible entries distributed and received. Prizewinners will be determined no later than June 30, 1996.

Sweepstakes open to residents of the U.S. (except Puerto Rico), Canada, Europe and Taiwan who are 18 years of age or older. All applicable laws and regulations apply. Sweepstakes offer void wherever prohibited by law. Values of all prizes are in U.S. currency. This sweepstakes is presented by Torstar Corp., its subsidiaries and affiliates, in conjunction with book, merchandise and/or product offerings. For a copy of the Official Rules governing this sweepstakes offer, send a self-addressed, stamped envelope (WA residents need not affix return postage) to: MILLION DOLLAR SWEEPSTAKES (III) Rules, P.O. Box 4573, Blair, NE 68009, USA.

SWP-TS94

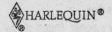 HARLEQUIN®  Silhouette®

The movie event of the season can be the reading event of the year!

Lights... The lights go on in October when CBS presents Harlequin/Silhouette Sunday Matinee Movies. These four movies are based on bestselling Harlequin and Silhouette novels.

Camera... As the cameras roll, be the first to read the original novels the movies are based on!

Action... Through this offer, you can have these books sent directly to you! Just fill in the order form below and you could be reading the books...before the movie!

48288-4	Treacherous Beauties by Cheryl Emerson		
		$3.99 U.S./$4.50 CAN.	☐
83305-9	Fantasy Man by Sharon Green		
		$3.99 U.S./$4.50 CAN.	☐
48289-2	A Change of Place by Tracy Sinclair		
		$3.99 U.S./$4.50CAN.	☐
83306-7	Another Woman by Margot Dalton		
		$3.99 U.S./$4.50 CAN.	☐

TOTAL AMOUNT	$
POSTAGE & HANDLING	$
($1.00 for one book, 50¢ for each additional)	
APPLICABLE TAXES*	$_____
<u>**TOTAL PAYABLE**</u>	$_____
(check or money order—please do not send cash)	

To order, complete this form and send it, along with a check or money order for the total above, payable to Harlequin Books, to: **In the U.S.:** 3010 Walden Avenue, P.O. Box 9047, Buffalo, NY 14269-9047; **In Canada:** P.O. Box 613, Fort Erie, Ontario, L2A 5X3.

Name: _____

Address: _____ City: _____

State/Prov.: _____ Zip/Postal Code: _____

*New York residents remit applicable sales taxes.
Canadian residents remit applicable GST and provincial taxes.   CBSPR

"HOORAY FOR HOLLYWOOD" SWEEPSTAKES

HERE'S HOW THE SWEEPSTAKES WORKS

OFFICIAL RULES — NO PURCHASE NECESSARY

To enter, complete an Official Entry Form or hand print on a 3" x 5" card the words "HOORAY FOR HOLLYWOOD", your name and address and mail your entry in the pre-addressed envelope (if provided) or to: "Hooray for Hollywood" Sweepstakes, P.O. Box 9076, Buffalo, NY 14269-9076 or "Hooray for Hollywood" Sweepstakes, P.O. Box 637, Fort Erie, Ontario L2A 5X3. Entries must be sent via First Class Mail and be received no later than 12/31/94. No liability is assumed for lost, late or misdirected mail.

Winners will be selected in random drawings to be conducted no later than January 31, 1995 from all eligible entries received.

Grand Prize: A 7-day/6-night trip for 2 to Los Angeles, CA including round trip air transportation from commercial airport nearest winner's residence, accommodations at the Regent Beverly Wilshire Hotel, free rental car, and $1,000 spending money. (Approximate prize value which will vary dependent upon winner's residence: $5,400.00 U.S.); 500 Second Prizes: A pair of "Hollywood Star" sunglasses (prize value: $9.95 U.S. each). Winner selection is under the supervision of D.L. Blair, Inc., an independent judging organization, whose decisions are final. Grand Prize travelers must sign and return a release of liability prior to traveling. Trip must be taken by 2/1/96 and is subject to airline schedules and accommodations availability.

Sweepstakes offer is open to residents of the U.S. (except Puerto Rico) and Canada who are 18 years of age or older, except employees and immediate family members of Harlequin Enterprises, Ltd., its affiliates, subsidiaries, and all agencies, entities or persons connected with the use, marketing or conduct of this sweepstakes. All federal, state, provincial, municipal and local laws apply. Offer void wherever prohibited by law. Taxes and/or duties are the sole responsibility of the winners. Any litigation within the province of Quebec respecting the conduct and awarding of prizes may be submitted to the Regie des loteries et courses du Quebec. All prizes will be awarded; winners will be notified by mail. No substitution of prizes are permitted. Odds of winning are dependent upon the number of eligible entries received.

Potential grand prize winner must sign and return an Affidavit of Eligibility within 30 days of notification. In the event of non-compliance within this time period, prize may be awarded to an alternate winner. Prize notification returned as undeliverable may result in the awarding of prize to an alternate winner. By acceptance of their prize, winners consent to use of their names, photographs, or likenesses for purpose of advertising, trade and promotion on behalf of Harlequin Enterprises, Ltd., without further compensation unless prohibited by law. A Canadian winner must correctly answer an arithmetical skill-testing question in order to be awarded the prize.

For a list of winners (available after 2/28/95), send a separate stamped, self-addressed envelope to: Hooray for Hollywood Sweepstakes 3252 Winners, P.O. Box 4200, Blair, NE 68009.

CBSRLS

OFFICIAL ENTRY COUPON

"Hooray for Hollywood"
SWEEPSTAKES!

Yes, I'd love to win the Grand Prize — a vacation in Hollywood —
or one of 500 pairs of "sunglasses of the stars"! Please enter me
in the sweepstakes!

This entry must be received by December 31, 1994.
Winners will be notified by January 31, 1995.

Name _____

Address _____ Apt. _____

City _____

State/Prov. _____ Zip/Postal Code _____

Daytime phone number _____
(area code)

Mail all entries to: Hooray for Hollywood Sweepstakes,
P.O. Box 9076, Buffalo, NY 14269-9076.
In Canada, mail to: Hooray for Hollywood Sweepstakes,
P.O. Box 637, Fort Erie, ON L2A 5X3.

KCH

OFFICIAL ENTRY COUPON

"Hooray for Hollywood"
SWEEPSTAKES!

Yes, I'd love to win the Grand Prize — a vacation in Hollywood —
or one of 500 pairs of "sunglasses of the stars"! Please enter me
in the sweepstakes!

This entry must be received by December 31, 1994.
Winners will be notified by January 31, 1995.

Name _____

Address _____ Apt. _____

City _____

State/Prov. _____ Zip/Postal Code _____

Daytime phone number _____
(area code)

Mail all entries to: Hooray for Hollywood Sweepstakes,
P.O. Box 9076, Buffalo, NY 14269-9076.
In Canada, mail to: Hooray for Hollywood Sweepstakes,
P.O. Box 637, Fort Erie, ON L2A 5X3.

KCH